Lies Untold

Kyra Leslie

*Our mission is to efficiently provide the world's finest, most comprehensive
book publishing service, enabling every author to experience success.
To find out how to publish your book, your way, and have it available
worldwide, visit us online at www.trafford.com*

Trafford rev. 1/6/2010

 www.trafford.com

North America & international
toll-free: 1 888 232 4444 (USA & Canada)
phone: 250 383 6864 ♦ fax: 812 355 4082

Dedicated to:
Cali Castillo and Robert G.

Acknowledgements

FIRST AND foremost, I would like to thank God for blessing me with the gift of writing and having the will to share my writing with others. I also thank him for instilling the faith, courage and preservance within myself to make my dream a reality.

I thank my mother, Troycia for being the amazing and inspirable woman that she is. Without her I would not be the woman that I have grown to be. To her, I give love and gratitiude for showing me how to be strong, independent, determined, and faithful. Because of her, I have learned patience, how to be a survivor of life with the cards that I have been dealt, and most importanly, how to be an amazing mother.

To my sister, JaResha and brother in law, Kevin, I thank you for pushing me when I didn't know how to push myself. For having the faith in my writing when at one point all I seen was just words on a page. For stepping in to help with my children when their fathers were "MIA"... which allowed me to see that I indeed had a purpose to pursue.

My 3 M's...Meara, Meauna, and Mekyle. I love you! Look, we did it. Without having you in my life, I would not know how to love as much while wanting and striving to provide for those who depend on me. You are my angels and let this be a message to you, "You can do all things through Christ that strengthens you."

To Nannie, thank you for instilling in me to always put God first in everything that I do. Thank you for helping me when I needed what you could only give...your knowledge, your prayers and your faith.

v

My love Randy, for stepping up to the plate and showing me the characteristics of a true man. For having my back in whatever decision I make, and for being my friend first and then mate. Thank you.

Pastor and Sis Prim, I thank you for continually lifting my family and self up in prayer. You are truly a blessing in our lives.

The Nelson family, you are my 2nd family! Thank you for your support and stepping up to the plate when I need you.

To Ed and Donovan for being who you are, which in turn allowed me to become who I am.

My special friends Melissa, Kedra, Dawn, Retha, Kenda, Kenny and Bobbie. In your own special way, you have each contributed to growth in my life. You have seen me evolve in a way that no one else has, while giving and sharing words of encouragement through the years that has enabled me to learn to deal with the ups and downs of life's experiences. Thank you and I love you.

Friends and associates at Truman who believed in me and was as eager for me to get this book published as I was for myself. Who gave me words of advice and a lending ear when it seemed as though it didn't seem as though this was going to happen when I wanted it to. Thank you, Katina R., Lisa S., Cynthia N., Julia H.,Tamika F., Terrail K., Robert S.,Trina, Sherri and others who lifted me up in joy. You all have touched my mind and heart in a remarkable way. You will never be forgotten.

Michael, I thank you for your patience as well as a cover illustration out of this world. We make a great team and this is only the beginning!

Bridget D., Words cannot express how grateful I am for your willingness to step up in a moments notice to edit what means the world to me (besides my babies of course.) You helped bring this book to life...I owe you.

To all of the single parents that have struggled while trying to raise your babies...Always know that as long as you stay faithful and put God first, anything is possible. Stay encouraged and focused.

Last but not least, I would like to thank the Trafford staff for working beside me on this amazing journey. Thank you.

"Lies Untold"

NO ONE would've have ever imagined that I'd be where I am in my life right now. Hell, I wouldn't blame them, with the life I had recently grown accustomed to.

Since the birth of my children, I had struggled. I didn't accept change, and decided that I never would. I was set on not allowing anyone to dictate how I lived my life. I figured I survived this long, so I had to be doing something right. I was sure that no one and nothing could change my mind--that is, until the night my life changed forever and I thought I was going to die. I vaguely remembered the exact details, but what I can recall made me grateful for the life I thought I hated.

"Twenty-five year old African-American female. Gunshot wound to the head by unknown suspect. B/P 60/40 palpable," a female voice calmly reported. I heard scrambling and movement all around me. They were moving quickly as if they didn't have much time to save my life. I couldn't see anything, and the words that were audible started to become distant. The voices were slowly fading away.

"B/P is dropping. We're losing her--she's coding! Everyone clear."

While struggling for every breath, it felt as though I was being lifted out of my body. I wanted so much to tell the doctors and nurses who were fighting to save my life that it wasn't my fault things turned out this way; I wanted to scream, "I deserve to live! I'm not a bad person, I just made wrong decisions!"

But I couldn't.

If I hadn't allowed greed to overcome my thoughts, I know things would be different and I wouldn't be struggling to live for my children.

Who would have figured that trying to provide for my kids by making a sacrifice--for just a few months--would jeopardize my life? Even though I was moonlighting as a prostitute, who would want to kill me, Jaelynn Stone?

I was a single, broke-as-hell, 24-year-old-mother with four children. None of my kids had any firsthand experience with the term "daddy." They all had different fathers except two of them, who were twins. Only one of three men knew we had a child together: Jason, the father of my oldest child, Sasha.

We were dating when I conceived, but then he got caught up in some crazy- ass drama that sent him to prison. I stuck by him for a couple of years, but I guess my love for him was not as strong as I thought. Over time, my letters to him became fewer and farther between, and I started canceling the monthly visits I promised him I'd make. Eventually, the collect calls stopped coming.

The twins' dad wasn't even my man; he was the boyfriend of my cousin, Keisha. We secretly messed around now and then when they had problems. I tried to break it off when it seemed like they were trying to take their relationship to the next level, but the night I decided to tell him that it was over was the same night I discovered I was pregnant.

I didn't want to ruin their relationship and become the black sheep of the family (although I was already halfway there, considering how my family judged my financial problems). So, I tried to do the right thing and tell him while we were alone.

When Keisha was at work, I surprised him with a visit and planned to tell him the news. He surprised me even more, informing me that we had to stop seeing each other since he and Keisha were engaged. Without a second thought, I distanced myself from him and moved on to someone else to cover up the pregnancy. Now, I try to keep my distance from that side of the family. They made it to the next level, alright...but they have kids who look just like mine.

After my fourth child, whose father I'm unsure of (although I've narrowed it down to three), I decided to make a change. Being broke had finally become depressing and tiresome, although I had been working in a department store. The pay was decent, and I was good at it—I even came close to being named assistant manager in the children's department—but it didn't exactly propel me past living paycheck to paycheck. As usual, I was constantly broke and struggling to make ends meet. My motivation to do something different (and profitable) really grew when Sasha started wanted to dress and like the other 2nd graders in her class. I wanted to make a change in my life, not only for me, but for them as well. I wanted to buy them nice clothes and toys—you know, the things that kids should have while growing up. Besides, my stupidity was not their fault. They deserved more than I had been able to give them since there were many times I didn't even have fifty cents to my name.

I often sat back and wondered how my plans for being successful and living the good life got derailed. I always dreamed I'd have a successful career, two wonderful kids, and an amazing husband who was my friend, lover, husband and soul mate. They say dream big and have big right? Well, I guess I didn't dream big enough, or peer pressure sucked me in before I finished.

In high school, I did well academically, participated in different activities, and at one time, was considered to be somewhat of a nerd. I had a few friends who were not exactly considered part of the "it" crowd, but were well liked by almost everyone. I guess, for me, that wasn't good enough--so I started hanging with the ones who were more popular and envied.

My first big break into the "newness" came when I was at the mall trying on a party outfit. A senior on the football team noticed me—at 5'4" and 120 pounds, I was pretty stacked, with thighs and a butt of steel—and told his friends that I had it going on (you know, for a "square"). Once he saw what I was working with, I jumped the express train to the "A" list, and began hanging out with the people that everyone wanted to hang with. My new friends and I frequented the mall, went to the movies, and then graduated to college parties. We met plenty of *fine*, well-to-do college brothas with their own places, and felt like we were grown along with them. Deep down, I knew I wasn't ready for what I was getting myself into, but I was having fun. Besides, I was too smart to end up like some of the other girls who didn't use their heads.

By the time I decided to get back on the right track (and slow down), it was too late: I was a baby having a baby. I stayed in denial for awhile, but reality set in during my third trimester. As the delivery grew nearer, everyone kept asking questions like, "Are you ready for all that pain? Will you have an epidural? Do you think your Lamaze classes were helpful? And, it was annoying. I just wanted to be left alone, because fear had finally kicked in. Initially, I thought Jason and I could actually make it work since we were so close. But once he was sentenced, I knew things would be different than what I had hoped for.

When Sasha was born, I lived at home with my parents, and still felt like a child although I had a baby of my own. Eventually, I started looking for a place but had no idea how I was going to afford living alone.

My parents tried to tell me how difficult working, attending school and caring for a baby would be for me. I knew they were right, and decided not to go back to school, at least for awhile. I figured I could get my G.E.D. and go to a community college when the time was right. (I hadn't thought about what would define "the right time," but figured when it came, I'd know.)

When I told my parents, they hit the roof—and made other plans.

"If you want to go, Jaelynn, that's fine," my mother cried. "But I'll be damned if I let you to take my grandchild out into a world that you can't handle!"

I was furious! If I wanted to move out, that was fine—as long as I left by myself? How could she make that decision for me? After that ultimatum, I decided to stay.

My first few months of motherhood were very difficult. I couldn't get adjusted to Sasha's schedule; she constantly woke up at night, and getting her back to sleep always seemed impossible. My mom helped me care for her pretty often.

My grades started dropping, and the friends I thought I had turned their backs on me. Tracy, a girlfriend of mine who forgave me after I left her to kick it with the popular kids, was one of the few who stuck by me. She got me out of the house to get some fresh air, and often stopped by to help when she could hear over the phone that I was getting stressed.

You'd think I'd have been even more cautious about sex, with Sasha's future to consider. But, I found myself pregnant again at 18 with the twins, and then again with my youngest.

A straight-shooter by nature, I asked my father point blank: "You're tired of carrying me, aren't you? You know I can't make it on my own, don't you?"

He was unable to look at me. While staring down at the paper he was reading he answered. "What makes you think that? You know that we would tell you."

"You're a damn lie. You think I'm pathetic. I didn't go to college like you planned—I broke the chain…daddy's little girl fucked up, huh?" I questioned.

He finally looked up in bewilderment.

"No, that's not the case. Look, Jaelynn--don't blame us for your short-comings. Yes, you've made mistakes, and yes, we have helped you often, but we can get through this."

"No one is putting any type of blame on you," my mother chimed in, "but things will change if you ever talk to your father or me like that again."

They never told me that they were getting fed up, but they didn't have to. I knew. Just because I was broke, didn't mean I was dumb too.

Not only did I have two successful parents, (my mother was an accountant and my father was an architect and real estate agent), I also had two older sisters, Monique and Jade, who were a year and a half apart. They were the best sisters anyone could've ever asked for. I often thought that I was different from them; it seemed as though they were too perfect to have the same blood as I did. The thoughts in my head constantly replayed when I realized how bad my life was becoming. If I had followed in their foot steps instead of straying to the path that I took, my life could've been where everyone including myself expected…happy and successful with children that I could take care of on my own. They supported me in almost every decision, even if they knew I was wrong. Their willingness to support eventually came to an end, though, as they grew tired of my broke ass always asking for money and food for the kids.

There was a time when those who knew us thought that the three of us were all going to one day be successful women who graduated from prestige black colleges, but of course I broke the chain when I became pregnant. Deep down, I knew I could have finished high school and gone to college (even with children), but at the time, I felt hopeless.

When my sisters moved away, I thought my world was going to end. We did everything together, and, other than Tracy, I didn't really have any outside friends.

Both sisters asked me to move away with them. When I became pregnant with Sasha, Monique begged me to move to Atlanta with her. She was doing well for herself professionally, and promised to help me get on the right track. "Once you have the baby," she said, "We can work on finding the right school for you, so you won't regret quitting school."

I decided to give it a chance and packed up all of my belongings, only to find out that my other sister wanted me to move in with her, too.

Jade attended law school in Texas and lived with her best friend from high school. They were both busy studying for their bar exams and worked part time, but also promised to help me with Sasha. So I wouldn't disappoint either of them, I declined to move with either of them and prayed that I would make it while staying home with Mom and Dad.

As time went on, my relationships with Monica and Jade suffered. They both disagreed with my decision to stay. They thought it was high time I moved out of our parents' house.

My family and I were so close at one time, but as I changed, our relationship changed, too. I became very defensive around them because it felt like they were trying to run my life and tell me how to take care of my kids. Even though they were often right, I grew distant. Following my lead, so did they.

Losing my safety net certainly opened my eyes.

The Meeting

WE MET at a comedy show at the downtown Improv Theater. I knew it was going to be a big turnout, and everyone would be dressed to impress. After a long search, I found a boutique in New York called Bebe on 100th and Fifth Ave. Since I didn't have room to splurge yet alone even go to a comedy show, I had to make a sacrifice and abstain from paying the light bill.

I, too, had to look delicious; just in case I crossed paths with "the one." I was certain that having a good man by my side was exactly what I needed and therefore, I did what I felt was needed to get one to look my way.

"Excuse me—can I get to that seat down there?" I asked, passing the little cutie in front of me, as I attempted to make my way to where Tracy was sitting.

Ordinarily, I'm not too fond of light-skinned men, but Brian was one sexy exception. He was tall, about 6'4," 200 pounds, slightly bow-legged, and I could tell he worked out. He had a low fade with a small goatee that accented those beautiful white teeth of his. He looked like one of those metrosexual brothas, the ones who get their monthly pedicures and manicures.

At first, I got a little pissed, since he didn't respond to me as quickly as I expected. I automatically assumed that he was an arrogant bastard and thought he knew he looked good, but just as I was about to write him off, he smirked and said, "Yeah, if you leave your number on the way down there."

My heart fluttered. He was too cute.

I tried to play coy, passing him by and acting like I wasn't inter-ested…but I jumped when I felt his hand rub the side of my thigh. Chills climbed my spine! I stopped, backed up, and then whispered in his ear, "The next time you try some shit like that, we'd better be alone."

Then, I took a pen out of my purse and wrote my name and number on his palm, mouthing "call me," as I made my way down the aisle to my seat.

As soon as I reached my seat, the show started. Midway through Cousin Terry's set, my cell phone rang. I assumed it was the babysitter, calling to say the kids were already acting like fools, which they some-times did when they were in the company of new people.

"Yes?" I answer, whispering. No response.

"Hello, is someone there?"

Still no response, so I hung up to check my incoming calls. The num-ber was one that I didn't know. I put the phone between my thighs for easier accessibility and shifted my attention back to the stage. The same number popped up, so I answered again.

"Hello?"

An unrecognizable male voice speaks: "Where are you going when you leave here?" Puzzled, I respond with a bit of an attitude. "Excuse me?"

He starts again, "You told me to call you didn't you? Or did you change your mind that quickly?"

Ah…Mr. Cutie.

I told him I had to go home to check on my kids, but it didn't seem to faze him. Instead of asking how many kids I had, he told me he un-derstood, and that he would call me the next day. I told him I would be looking for his call and to make sure that he didn't keep me waiting too long.

My girlfriend Tracy, who came to the show with me, looked at me like she knew I was up to something—but she didn't say anything. We'd been friends forever, and, at times it seemed as though we could read each others' minds. We rarely wasted our time explaining our-selves to each other. I leaned over and whispered to her, "Girl, I'll tell you later."

We were the same age but had totally different outlooks on life and relationships. Tracy had a commitment phobia, and kept an assort-ment of "man candy" at her disposal. Growing up, her mother had several bad relationships, and Tracy promised herself that she'd never go through the same headaches. She figured if she had several friends who could satisfy her "sweet tooth" cravings, what was the use of having just one?

The only problem I had with her way of thinking was that a couple of her so-called "candies" were married. I always reminded her that it wasn't right to sample other peoples' goodies and reminded her to think when she decided to get married. She'd often tell me "If I can't please my man the way I should, he needs to get some elsewhere, but remember--I'm not getting married." After many attempts to get her to listen to reason, I learned to leave her alone. Some things you just have to learn the hard way.

Cousin Terry is still on stage making jokes trying to convince the audience that he's the reason Mike, the headliner, is so famous. He said it's a shame that Mike is making more money, since he's the one who started it all.

"For real ya'll, they had a talent show and needed some wannabe comedians. I thought my cousin was pretty okay doing stand-up, so I convinced him try it. I told him to just do it for fun to see if he liked it, and here he is: damn-near a millionaire and loving it. For real: ya'll look at this shit! Here I am, opening for him, making a little bit of nothing. Hell, as a matter a fact, I ain't making a damn thing 'cause I'm his cousin and he expects me to do this." He goes on to mumble under his breath, "With his cheap ass."

The laughter was uproarious. Cousin Terry was just as funny as Mike.

Tracy leans over and gains my attention by telling me something that I thought would make me piss in my seat.

"Hey Jay, look at that brother down there who just sat down," Tracy said, nudging my arm with her elbow and looks at Brian down the way.

"Uh huh," I said, trying to act uninterested.

"No girl, you must be looking at the wrong man, 'cause you'd be saying more than that, if you saw him. I'm 'bout to make my way down there to get better acquainted." I grabbed her hand.

"Wait a minute! I already did that. You're late, sister girl." She looks at me with one eyebrow raised.

"What?!" she screamed, and then remembered where were at, and lowered her voice.

"When did this happen?" Trying to keep from smiling, I tell her about our meeting, and just to make her furious, wink at her.

"He's about to be *my* candy; just wait and see."

As she tries to get back into the show, she looks over at me expecting me to tell her more. As much as I wanted to tell her, I kept my composure, to refrain from laughing and continued looking ahead.

After awhile, I get up to go to the bathroom to take a look at myself and freshen up a little bit. I knew the turnout was big, but I had no idea just how many people really had came out to see the show, until I got up to leave the auditorium. It seemed as though all eyes were on me, and surprisingly, it was kinda scary even though I used to love being the center of attention. It felt like I was being followed by millions of eyes from the time I left my seat, to the time I left the auditorium. As I was walking out, I started to wonder if I had something on me, or if my outfit wasn't fitting right despite getting Brian's attention. Maybe on the other hand it was what I expected, and I just looked that damn good. After all, Tracy would've told me if I looked a mess.

As I'm leaving the bathroom, I hear Brian call my name. I slowly walk towards him and try to keep a steady gait, but it was difficult because I was so nervous. There was something about this man that made me want to jump him right then and there! As I get closer to him, he takes my hand and we start walking down the hall towards the auditorium. He tells me that he saw me before we actually met, and had plans on approaching me anyway. At this point I'm wondering how many other women he's approached besides me, but then decide to leave it alone. It's not like we had plans on getting married or anything. Hell, I would've been satisfied to just go on a few dates with him and get wined, dined and laid.

We walked, talked, and laughed as if we had known each other for awhile, almost forgetting that we came to see a comedy show. As we re-entered the auditorium, he stops and asks, "What are your plans when you leave here?" I laugh aloud and remind him, that he already asked me that.

He sheepishly grins and says, "Oh yeah, the babies." I nod and tell him that I promise to call him tomorrow. I wanted to say something that was not exactly the way I normally handled things, but with him, the temptation was hard to resist. My plan before going back to my seat was to go home with him, but I knew it was best to go home to the kids as planned, and alone at that.

When I returned to my seat, Tracy gave me the "I know you" look. I smiled and said, "Nothing happened—yet," and watched the remainder of the show.

Images of Two

THE SMELL of ham awakened me, and as I struggled to open my eyes. I noticed that, as usual, two of my four were children lying in bed with me: one of the twins Shaun, and my youngest Shauvon. Of all of my children, they were the most spoiled. It wasn't as if I gave them more attention than my other two, I just babied them more and gave them lots of love and attention. I knew they wanted toys just like other children, but my love was what they appreciated most.

My other two, Sasha and Shaunice, the other twin, were the independent ones. I understood Sasha being that way because she was older than her siblings, but Shaunice, seemed to be a lot like me: she had a mind of her own and whatever she set her mind into doing, she did.

Sasha was the chef in the house and was always cooking and experimenting with whatever we had, which most of the time wasn't much. She would often tell me that it was okay if we weren't able to have meat every night because she had one day thought of being a vegetarian anyway.

"I heard that it was healthier to not eat meat anyway, Momma. The kids may not understand, but they will when they get older," she would say.

For breakfast, she scrambled up some cheesy eggs, and warmed up some ham. It was still pretty early, and I had no idea why she was up already, but whatever the case, I was glad she was making breakfast since I was dead tired from the night before.

"Momma, I made you breakfast since you got in late," she said eagerly as she stood over me with a tray in her hands. "There's enough in there for the kids too." Along with the eggs and ham, she also had a bowl of cereal with milk to the brim and a tall glass of orange juice.

"Umm, breakfast in bed? Thank you, baby! Do you want me to fix you something different?" I asked, already knowing what her response was going to be.

"Mm hmm. I would like some pancakes with strawberry syrup!" She eagerly replied.

I smiled and said, "Okay, let me eat this before it gets cold and then it'll be my turn to fix you something."

After eating, I fixed Sasha the pancakes she wanted, got the other kids started on their breakfast, and prepared to take a nice relaxing shower to wake myself up. I turned the hot water on in the shower, and went to grab my clothes. Just as I went to step in, the phone rings. It was Tracy.

"Hey heffa, I had to call to make sure you didn't go back out and stay gone after I dropped you off, you freak." We both laughed while I landed on my back in my bed. I told her my babies were more important than some one night stand, but did mention that I had plans to call him so we could go out for dinner or something.

"Hey let me call you back girl, I'm about to get in the shower. Besides, I know your ass don't want anything and you was just calling to be nosey." I smiled as I hung up.

The bathroom was hot and steamy and the whole time that I was in there, Brian constantly occupied my mind. I imagined our first date and how perfect it was going to be. I couldn't wait to feel how good it was going to be when he satisfied this ancient tomb of mine.

As I lusted for his touch while visualizing the two of us together, my nipples hardened with each thought of him. I knew it was too early for me to be visualizing him as I was, but my attraction to him was like no other and there was nothing I could do to shake it off. I closed my eyes and imagined him there with me. I found myself touching myself and began to feel the passion I imagined between the two of us. As I reached the height of my glory, I heard a knock at the door which quickly woke me up from my erotic, romancing touch.

"Momma, I'm still hungry..." Shaun wines.

"Okay baby, I'm getting out. I'll be right there." Damn!

Saturdays were the days the kids and I would do the things they wanted to do. We'd make breakfast together and they would find change around the house to "pay" for their breakfast. For me, it was my attempt at teaching them responsibility, but for them, it was their I-Hop breakfast day. They would often order their favorite, pancakes with blueberries, bacon and strawberry milk. Unbeknownst to them, it was my favorite, too. It made me feel like a kid all over again, and when they had fun, I had more. The money they found would go into a piggy bank, and then on Sunday they'd put it in church for their offering when we actually made it to church.

Right after breakfast, we'd watch cartoons for about an hour, and then if the car was willing to start and the weather was nice, we'd go to the park or take a joy ride around the city. We'd often take trips to the mall and window shop until we got bored. Although most of the time I couldn't afford to buy them anything, they still enjoyed getting out and fantasizing about what they would ask for if I did have the money. There were times that I would get depressed and become angry at myself for getting myself into the predicament I was in, but I quickly came around, after realizing that it gave us a chance to have fun while spending time out of the house. It allowed them to see that despite our financial situation, we could still find ways to enjoy life, and be happy with one another.

After cartoons, we usually took baths, dressed according to the weather and headed out. But just as we were about to head out the door on this particular day, Brian calls.

"I've been thinking about you all morning, Ms. Lady. What's up with that?" he questioned.

I smile from ear to ear, and respond sheepishly "I don't know, but it's good to hear. Believe it or not, I had you on my mind as well. Maybe we have a good connection."

"For sure," he says. "So what's up with you for the day? I thought maybe we could go and grab lunch or something," he asks.

It surprised me that he would ask so nonchalantly, without giving me a heads up. He knew that I had my babies and should've known that I needed to find a sitter first, but I guess I should've been grateful that he asked in the first place.

"Brian, I told you I had children, so you know I need to plan ahead. Besides, we already have our day planned. I'm sorry."

"No need to be sorry, I should've thought about that anyway. Well, how about you give me a call later so we could talk? Then maybe we could decide on where and when we want our first date to be."

I happily agreed and noticed that when I hung up the phone, my son was looking at me. He wondered who was on the other end, making me smile and blush.

"Momma, who was that?" Shaun was my little protector and took his "little man of the house" role very seriously. Although he was only four, he knew how to hold the fort down. If at anytime I had a friend over, or if someone new called the house, he made a point to find out who he was.

Now don't get me wrong, I didn't ordinarily invite anyone over to the house. I didn't think that it was acceptable for my kids to see everyone that I meet, but if I've known someone for awhile, I invite them over to hang out and that's it. Spending the night, of course, was not allowed. I believed in setting a good example for my kids.

"That was a friend of mine, baby," I told him.

"Your boyfriend, Momma?" he asked with one eye half closed as if something was irritating it.

"No...but if it was, what are you going to do about it?" I questioned him while leaping at him and tickling him once I had him in my arms. I tickled him so hard he started coughing and almost threw up on me. When he started whining, I stopped and held him in my arms as if he was just born. As I was holding him, I thought about how amazing it was that I loved them so much and how I would do anything to provide the life that I owed them as their mother.

Then he asks the question he's asked before:

"Momma, where's our daddy?"

Before answering, I inhaled and exhaled even longer. I offered my usual lie, saying that he moved out of town. His response had always been "Why is he out of town?" or "When is he coming back?" but this time, his response changed. He asked if he could go to see him.

I wondered how long I could keep feeding the twins lies about their father. After all, they were four and getting older and more curious. Next time, Shaun just may ask for his number.

I know that if I actually told Robert he would be mad and raise hell since I've kept his children from him. I do think he would try to do right by them—and me. He was a good person despite the love triangle he found himself in. Unlike Sasha's father, I don't think he had a bad bone in his body.

James was the worst out of all that I had dated. He dropped out of high school in the tenth grade and never held a job. I was surprised at how we crossed paths since I was hanging with the college brothas at the time. He should have been nowhere near college grounds, but he just so happened to arrive at one of the parties I was at. I caught his eye, as well as something else that I probably don't need to explain.

While we were together, he had always said that he wasn't going to work for the white man, so he decided to sell drugs.

I had a problem with the way he made money while destroying the lives of others; but eventually looked past his shortcomings since I enjoyed spending it as fast as he made it.

Even though I feared for my life when I was with him, I also felt like I was on top of the world. I didn't have to want for anything and although my parents made good money and spoiled me with whatever I wanted, his money was different. With him, I actually got a chance to hold some. I had never seen as much money with anyone as I did with him, and if anyone ever hinted that he would eventually run out of it, he just laughed at them while reminding them that haters never got on top.

Rumor had it that, during a drug bust, he killed two policemen and injured one. He had never been honest enough to convey that to me, and left me with no choice but to believe the rumors. Murder was completely unexplainable in my eyes, whether intentional or accidental. Therefore, I found myself backing away realizing that this shortcoming could not be ignored.

Now don't get me wrong, James was a wonderful boyfriend, and when he wasn't taking care of business, he was taking care of me. He didn't take any shit off of anyone either, and although I was scared of the life that he chose to live, I felt comfortable knowing that if anything went down, he was definitely going to hold the fort down. Every now and then, someone who would try to be Billy Bad Ass and attempt to run up on him, but I can say that after that one attempt, they never tried again.

I strongly believe that, although relationships don't always work out the way we want them to, kids deserve to have both parents, whether they are both in the home or not, so when I learned that prison was going to be James new home for awhile, I knew that I was going to have my hands full. Not only did I realize that life was going to be hard, but I became angry that someone snitched on him taking away my comfort zone.

Because of Brian's call, we got off to a late start. When I finally got it together so we could head to the car, the phone rang as we headed out the door.

"Momma *come on*, you don't have to answer it," whined Sasha.

"I know baby, 'cause you are!" I said with a smile on my face.

She ran to get the phone and within seconds yelled outside that it was for me. When I didn't get any response after asking her who it was, I decided to rush in to see for myself and told the kids to stay put on the porch.

"Hello?" I answered.

"Hi, is the woman of the house available?" a young man had asked. I had no idea who he was and started to hang up the phone, but curiosity kept me on.

By the sound of his voice, I figured he was a white professional male in his mid 30s. Bill collector was my first intuition, but I assumed that they wouldn't be calling on a Saturday.

"Who's calling?" I asked as I started to hear a chuckle on the other end.

"Hey baby girl, it's me again." It was Brian.

"Brian! I can't believe you had me thinking you were some damn bill collector, why'd you do that!" I exclaimed. "I was about to hang up on your ass," I laughed.

"Now, why is that? You shouldn't be dodging any bill collectors. Just pay 'em so you won't have to worry about them calling your house."

If only he knew. At one time I had pretty decent credit and even had a couple of credit cards, but after the twins, the good credit thing went down the drain. I started charging all kinds of stuff, because I didn't have the cash to pay for half of the things the kids needed while I was waiting for the next payday. I always said that as soon as I got paid, I would pay on the items that I charged so it wouldn't add up. Unfortunately, when that time came around, something else came up and eventually, I found myself in a hole.

"I wish it was that easy. You seem to forget that I am a single parent with four kids, just barely making ends meet while working in a department store."

Catching myself after the fact about the info that I had just conveyed to him, I realized that now, he may have thought I had too much baggage for him to want to be involved. So I waited for him to say "I'll holla." Surprisingly, he didn't.

"Well look, shit happens to the best of us, I guess that means that when we get to know each other a little better and start being together, I'll have to help you out with a little somethin' somethin' to get you back on track."

I felt that what I was hearing was too good to be true, and thanked God for sending me a man who was willing to help a sister out.

"Anyway, we'll come to that point as time progresses. I was actually calling back to see if you would like to go out to dinner with me tomorrow?"

"Tomorrow?" I thought. Hell I wanted to see him tonight, especially after he told me he was willing to help a sista out; I wanted to get this show on the road! Forget getting to know one another. I felt like telling him, give it to me now and you can get to know me later. But of course I didn't.

"Yeah, tomorrow's fine. But umm…" I paused for a minute.

"I was actually wondering if we could go ahead and meet up later on…that is if you don't mind." I stated.

There was silence as if I had caught him off guard. It was killing me that it took him longer than I had imagined to answer so I chimed in before I could have him reject me

"You know what, never mind. You asked me earlier and I said no, so I completely understand if…"

He cut me off. "If what? That's cool. How about 5:30 or 6:00?"

I grinned sheepishly trying to hide the excitement in my voice when I answered him.

"Okay, sounds good. Thank you. What should I wear? Something casual or dressy?" I asked trying to sound as sexy as possible.

"Let's say something casual. I want you to be comfortable."

I made sure I hung the phone up first since I felt like I was about to explode. I didn't want him to hear how excited I really was about this date. I started dancing and twirling around the living room like I had just won a million dollars.

As I gained my composure, I noticed that the kids were back in the house and were watching as I acted like a teenager.

"I'm sorry, ya'll. Momma got a little excited. Are you ready to go?" I didn't have to ask more than once because before I finished, they were already out the door.

While we were in the car, I asked what they wanted to do. The younger kids wanted to play, while Sasha insisted that we go to the mall. I told them that we would do both, as long as they remembered that I didn't have any extra money, and I couldn't be buying everything in sight.

"Momma, why don't you ever have any money?" asked Shaunice.

"Things happen baby, but you know what? That's all going to change one day."

"What day?" she asked.

"The day Momma gets back in school. I'm going back to school so I can get a better job, and then have more money for us!" I tried to say with enthusiasm. I knew that's what I wanted to do, but believing I could actually do it was the tricky part.

"School?" she questioned, "Momma you're too old to go to school. Only kids like us are supposed to go to school."

"Baby, you don't understand this now, but always remember: you're never too old to go to school," I said.

"But you already know how to read and you know your ABCs," Shaun cuts in, "so what else do you have to learn?"

As I try to keep from laughing, I tell him a lot more, and that he'll see when he gets older. I guess he was satisfied with that answer, because he didn't ask any more questions.

I just knew that whatever it was that I needed to do to help us get by; I was going to do not only for them, but for myself as well.

The First Date

I DIDN'T HAVE to worry about fixing dinner since we ran into an old friend of mine—Michelle, who offered to treat us to McDonald's. She said she was about to take her little girl there to play and she figured we could catch up on some things while they played. I was grateful that she offered to pay for our meal; that way, I had extra money for Sunday dinner.

I hadn't seen her since high school and was actually amazed at the transformation. She used to look homely, not like the other girls that I hung out with, but now you could tell that life had been good for her. I guess people are right when they say that money could do that for you since it was obvious she had more than her share.

She mentioned that she had been married, had only one child and was doing well for herself. She said she divorced her husband a couple of years later when she caught him cheating with her best friend.

"Jae, he was my all in all and I was truly submissive to him. I tried to forgive him to make our marriage work, but it wasn't worth it. He deceived me and broke our wedding vows," she confided. "I continuously imagined them together and couldn't take it any longer."

She began telling me how he ruined what she once thought was the perfect marriage.

"One week, I had to go out of town on a business trip. He usually tagged along when I went away, but this particular time, he decided to stay. He said he had some important business to take care of at home.

Girl, I knew it was kind of odd that he couldn't get away—being that he has his own business and could have taken the work with him--but I guess I ignored the signs," she struggled to continue.

Her meeting was cut short because of a family emergency of one of her co-workers. She didn't call her husband to tell him she was coming home, hoping to surprise him while their daughter was at the babysitter. She figured they would have time to enjoy each other for a few hours before picking her up. Instead found her best friend's car parked in the driveway.

"I went into the house trying not to assume the worst since they claimed that they weren't too fond of each other in the first place."

Tears welled in her eyes and I reached out my hand to her while trying to find a napkin.

She shook her head, refusing the napkin and letting me know that she was okay and didn't need my sympathy. She even managed a faint smile.

"She had been telling me for years that my husband was not the man for me and that I deserved better. I should have known that she was after him herself by the way that she constantly tried to make me find the bad in him. I should have listened to my gut, but I felt that if I did what he asked of me, he would remain happy and so would I."

"I stepped inside the house, I noticed that hers shoes were at the bottom of the stairs and other parts of her clothing—including her panties—were making a trail to our bedroom."

She assumed that she was going to find them in their bed together, but she walked into the bathroom and found them having sex in their shower.

I felt so bad for her, as she began crying uncontrollably. I couldn't tell her that it was going to be alright, because I had never been where she was. One thing I did know was that I hated him for her.

It made me think of Tracy and how, now more than ever, I wanted to get through to her about dating someone else's man. I wanted to prevent her from doing to someone else what this woman was going through.

Despite the infidelity and divorce, she said that she finally found herself and went back to college to do what she had always wanted to do which was get her law degree. For the first time that evening, she became joyous when talking about how she claimed her victory while making more money and living a life of peace not only for herself, but daughter as well. Hearing her story gave me hope that I too could overcome what I was going through

It was getting late and I had things to do, so we exchanged numbers, and told each other that we were going to keep in touch. I had told her that she was a strong woman, and a damn good person to not give them what they both deserved.

"Girl look, another woman would've done something so crazy that neither one of them would have ever been the same."

By the time we got home, we were all worn out, but I was determined not to allow my exhaustion ruin my time with Brian. The twins and my youngest were asleep, so I had Sasha help me put them to bed.

After getting the kids in bed, I figured that Sasha would be headed to bed as well. I went to my room, turned the radio on and started my bath water so I could freshen up before spending time with Brian.

Before stepping into the tub, a noise from the other room caught my attention and I went to check it out. I wasn't sure what it was, or where it was coming from, but followed the direction of the noise. To my surprise, I found Sasha lying on the couch crying with her head buried in a pillow.

"What's the matter baby?" I asked with tears starting to form in my eyes while I placed my hand on her back. My heart sunk and I felt a knot in the pit of my stomach. I began to think of what could have possibly happened while we were out. Why hadn't I noticed that something was bothering her? How could I have been too focused on myself and my needs rather than hers?

She didn't budge and continued to sob harder and louder. After I stroked her back and hair for a few minutes, her crying ceased. She sat up and put her arms around me as if she hadn't seen me for days. My mind raced uncontrollably; I worried that someone had done something to her while I was talking with Michelle at McDonald's.

I felt nauseous at the thought of someone hurting my child. Then I found out that someone wasn't just anybody, it was me.

Sasha told me that her friends at school were talking about dressing alike on Monday, and had decided to go to the mall to get an outfit from a trendy store called Sanaiz Styles. She had seen it earlier when we were browsing, and told me that was the reason she wanted to go to the mall in the first place. She wanted so bad to ask me if she could have it, but remembered that I told them that I didn't have any money, and to not ask for anything.

The outfit was fifteen dollars, and it broke my heart to know that I couldn't afford to buy my baby a fifteen dollar outfit so she could dress like her friends. The worst part was that she knew I couldn't afford it, so instead of asking and making me upset, she kept quiet and begged for it in her thoughts. Not only was I hurt that she was hurting, but I was more hurt that she felt that she could keep the peace by keeping quiet when she knew she really didn't want to, something a seven-year-old shouldn't have to do.

"Tell you what. I don't know how, but I'll try my best to get that outfit for you tomorrow okay? And Sasha, promise that you will never keep anything from me again. It is my responsibility to provide for you regardless of the circumstances, and from here on out, momma will do just that." I said trying to form a smile of my own.

She stopped crying and looked at me with thanks in her eyes.

"Thank you Momma, I love you so much!" she said, hugging the life out of me.

With tears in my eyes, I told her that I loved her too and walked to my room after she excitedly ran to hers. Not knowing where I was going to get the money, I went to the bathroom to take my bath and got into the tub in a different mood and frame of mind.

The candles I had gotten out earlier to relax with (while trying to think of the different ways I could seduce Brian), would now have to be put away. I felt like filling the rest of the tub with my tears and crying myself to sleep. Maybe I could drown in my sorrow.

Then, reality set in. I still had company coming.

I quickly took my bath and prayed that God would help me find a way. I then removed myself from the tub to get dressed for my date and hoped that my make up would hide the distress on my face. While finishing up, Tracy walked in.

"Sorry I'm late; I had a little dilemma at the furniture store. What's up chic? You ready for your date?" she asked, peering at the clothing I had laid out on the bed.

She walked over to the clothes that were neatly arranged on the bed and looked at me and them before returning her eyes to me.

"Hmm...looks like somebody is out to get a little somethin' somethin'. And look, you even got your hooker shoes out!" she excitedly whispered.

I pushed her out of the way, trying not to laugh since I knew she was right.

"Look, Sis—I ain't even mad at you, 'cause the brotha is fine!"

While snatching the shirt she had picked up off the bed, I attempted to change the subject.

"So, did you find what you were looking for? What color did you decide on?"

Tracy was remodeling her living room since she received her quarterly bonus check at the Post Office. At first, she asked me to help pick out a style and color, but then changed her mind because she wanted it to be a surprise.

"I think so. You'll see it soon—and girl, you will really be surprised."

She left the room, but then quickly returned, because she could tell something was wrong.

"What's going on, Jae? Something ain't right." she demanded.

Trying to refrain from crying again and ruining my make-up, I sat on the bed and told her about what happened.

"Damn boo, what can I do to help? What outfit is it? I'll get it for her." She replied.

I couldn't hold back. My make-up was ruined.

"Thanks, but it's not that simple. Look at my life, Tracy. What have I done? I can't take care of my kids. Hell, I don't know if I can take care of myself." I paused. "I swear, if it wasn't for them...I'd do something I know I would regret."

"You're definitely not thinking sensibly. You know whatever you need, I'll get. Come on, Jae—you've come too far to give up now."

She hugged me awhile and then held my face in her hands. "Look, hold your head up and keep the faith. I'm here whenever you need me. Now look: you better go get ready for this man so you can have a damn good time. And I suggest you hurry up before he gets the impression that you have issues. I already know that you do," she said laughing, "but it's for him to find out on his own that you do."

I laughed with her and thanked her for having my back. I didn't want him to think of me as a whore, but I was sure going to give him something to look at even if our date wound up being the first and the last.

When Brian arrived, he made a big, lasting impression. His sports car turned many heads in the neighborhood. I even thought about riding with him instead of driving my own and following him.

"Why don't you feel comfortable riding with me?" he asked.

I began to stutter in an attempt to plead my case.

"No, it's not *that*, I just...I...I feel more comfortable this way."

"Oh, so you think I'm some type of mass murderer?" he asks, then chuckles to relieve the tension he knew was building up inside of me. "I'm just messing with you baby girl, I completely understand."

Letting out a sigh of relief, I ask, "Do you really? I just..."

"Want to be careful," he cuts me off.

I reply, "Yes, you know there are some really crazy people in the world."

"Yeah I know. I'm one of those people." He half-heartedly smiles, giving me a look to make me wonder if he was serious or joking.

I become speechless—and uncomfortable. As I wonder if I should continue on with this date, he starts laughing.

"Baby girl, lighten up. I'm just kidding."

I tell him, "I hope so," and head out the door to get in my car.

I didn't want to go somewhere I was unfamiliar with, so I suggested Applebee's. I told him there was one close to my house, and he proceeded to follow me.

I didn't tell him that I had an acquaintance who worked there, but I knew that if I felt uncomfortable at any point, I could get out of staying. I thought that it would be good to have a plan in place in case the date started going in a direction I didn't want it to go.

As we waited for our food, we engaged into casual conversation about our interest, and different places that we've traveled outside of Kansas City. There have only been a couple of places that I've been fortunate enough to visit, but since he asked, I entertained it.

When I told him about the two placed I'd been, it surprised me that he was able to keep a straight face.

"Okay, you can laugh now. I won't feel bad."

"Laugh at what? Your adventures...nah, I'm good."

"You don't find it amusing that I haven't experienced much life outside of Kansas?" I questioned as I bit down on my straw.

"Nope. It is what it is. Maybe you just don't like to travel. As for me, I love it. I have to respect that people are different."

I wanted to ask about some of the places he had mentioned, but figured it wouldn't do me any good since I'd probably never get to see them anyway.

"It must be nice to have the luxury of traveling."

He shrugged his shoulders and took a sip of his water. "Yeah it's cool, but it would've been better if it was more for leisure than work."

I didn't want to get too personal and ask what type of work he did just yet, so I left it alone and changed the subject.

"I have to admit, this is nice. I thought I'd be a little nervous and out of sorts since this is the first date that I have been on in a while, but I can honestly say I feel at ease and relaxed, it feels as if we've already met and hung out before. Thank you." I said softly while looking at him and trying to read his expression.

"Good," he replies. "It's not a good thing when you're walking on egg shells, trying to avoid saying the wrong thing…I mean, everyone has jitters when going out with someone new, but when you're not being yourself, you could mess up a nice date by not letting the other person see you for who you really are, you know?"

Before I could comment, the waiter arrives with our salads. As we prepare to eat, Brian surprisingly grabs my hand, gives me a wink, and starts to bless the food. He gave thanks for allowing us to have the food we had before us, and for giving him the opportunity to be sitting in front of a beautiful lady.

Following his lead, I immediately began praying myself. I quietly gave thanks for the food and for allowing our paths to cross.

"Your salad okay?" he asks.

With my mouth full, I nod my head and mumble "Mm hmm," slightly embarrassed.

Then, our entrées arrived. Between taking bites of our meals, we continued our lets- get-to-know-each-other-better conversation, while deciding if we were going to do what we both wanted to do, which was call it a evening and go back to his place.

From what I heard, he seemed to have his life together just the way he wanted and was thankful for being able to have the things he had. He occasionally mentioned that he thought his life would be better if he had a lady to enjoy his success with, but until he found the one he was looking for, he would be content with what he had.

As much as I wanted, I didn't question him about what he was looking for (and if he thought I could be her). I figured if we were to go out on another date, I would find that out in due time, especially if I showed him that I could do what every man wanted their woman to do.

As we finished our meal, he asked if I wanted to indulge in dessert. Lord knows I did since it had been awhile that I had the luxury of being taken out and treated like a lady. I wanted to take advantage of every opportunity in front of me, since who knew when it would happen again?

"You know, as tempting as it sounds, I believe I'll pass" I said, kicking myself..

"Are you sure? You could always take it home with you, what about the babies, you think they may want something?" he asked.

Okay, now I was hooked. Not only did he take me out and impress me with what he had going on in his life, but he reeled me in when he thought about my kids.

"Nah, I think they're okay. Thanks for asking."

"You know Ms. Jae, you are a beautiful young lady and I bet men are waiting in line to be with you, so why are you single?"

I start to blush and allow a soft giggle to escape before realizing that I didn't answer.

"Seriously, you have to be dating someone," He continued trying to see which direction I was going to allow this to go.

I honestly didn't know if he was asking a question or making a comment. I attempted to play it off in hopes that I could do what I was good at: change the subject. I wasn't afraid of letting him know that I was single, I just didn't want him to feel that he could have me just when he wanted me. This body hadn't been touched the way I wanted it to be touched in years—but he didn't need to know that just yet.

"Forget about me, the question is, why are you not dating anyone? You seem to have everything else that you want—why not the perfect woman?" I shot back.

He looked at me while biting his lower lip, and let out a sigh.

"I haven't found the woman who is equally yoked with me. That's what I'm waiting for." He leaned back in his chair.

"I'm tired of being with someone just to be with them. I want us to have common interests, I want us to be able to finish each other's sentences, I want her to love the way I love. I haven't found that yet, so I am where I am...alone."

What was I supposed to say after that rehearsed line? I decide to tell him a lie of my own. He didn't have to know everything about me just yet.

"Well...I have friends that I occasionally meet up with from time to time. Nothing serious."

"Friends?" he questions.

"Yeah, ones that I talk to now and then, or might go out with for a drink with when I'm bored and need someone to hang out with." I don't elaborate any further.

Hesitantly, he asks, "So...are you not looking for more than friendship?"

I respond slowly. "I'd be willing to consider more if a good man comes my way. He'd have to be good to my kids and me. He'd have to be a respectful family man, and we'd have to be friends first."

Before I could add more, he cuts me off.

"Alright friend, we'll see where this friendship takes us. Sound good?" he smiles.

"Sounds good."

While walking to the car, I apologized for being in a hurry, and told him that I had to run to the mall. Like a gentleman, he offered to drive me and bring me back afterwards.

I found the outfit that Sasha described and asked the Sanaiz Styles salesperson if she would hold the outfit until Sunday. Brian overheard.

"Not trying to be nosey, but why don't you just get it now so you won't have to come back?" he asked.

"Well… I want to make sure it's the right size." I lied.

"Tell you what, if it is, I'll come with you to bring it back. Ma'am, please go ahead and ring it up." He pulled out his wallet.

Pushing his hand away, I stand up for myself, "I can't have you do this...I got it." I pulled out my wallet, knowing it that had less than ten dollars in it.

"Please, I want to," he said, encouraging me to leave it in my purse.

I gratefully relented, whispering in his ear, "Thanks again."

After leaving the mall, we headed to a bar to hang out for awhile longer. I decided to have a daiquiri, but ended up having a little bit more than that. Due to only having a drink every once and awhile, I limit my drinks when out with strangers. Fortunately for him, it was obvious that I broke that rule.

Since the bar was only a few minutes from Applebee's we decided that he would take us there and then take me back to my car later, but since it was obvious that I was in no place to drive myself home, we agreed for me to go back to his place so I could let some of the liquor wear off.

Before getting out of his car, I told him that regardless of the state of mind I was in, it didn't mean for him to try to do what he thought he might get away with it.

"Hey, Ms. Lady, I didn't bring you here to take advantage of you. When we were at the bar, you asked if you could rest at my place before you went home because you didn't want to drive. If you've changed your mind, I'm more than glad to take you back to your car and follow you to your place, or I can call you a taxi."

Needless to say, I followed his fine ass up to his place.

When I walked into his place, I seemed to sober up immediately.

I was more than impressed with what I walked into. Not only was it a condo, but it had a contemporary look that showed a woman had something to do with the set up. You could tell that no kids had stepped foot in it and it was almost hard to believe that he was a bachelor like he said he was.

"This doesn't look like a bachelor's pad to me," I said, making myself comfortable.

"Well it is. Just because I'm a man, doesn't mean I can't have style and surround myself with nice things. I mean, I have to admit I didn't pick everything out by myself... I did have a little help from the ladies who work in the places that I bought my things from."

Apologetically, I manage, "You have good taste. Damn, I'm almost jealous 'cause it looks better than mine."

I slowly stroll into his bedroom and plop down on the bed engaging myself in the softness of his pillow top mattress.

"Do you live alone?" I question as I take in the scent of lavender and chamomile.

"Yes I do," he smirks.

"Why did you smirk like that? Did 'Ms. Lady' hit a nerve?" I smirk back.

"No, not at all...you just happen to be very curious. There are times when my partner stops through for a day or two to get away from his chic, but other than that, it's me by my lonesome."

I immediately wonder if he's on the down low, but instead of further investigating the issue, I leave well enough alone. Besides, I wasn't ready to be put out, since I just got ready to see what he was all about.

"How long have you lived here?" I asked while sitting up.

"About nine months. Why all the questions? I feel like you're inter-rogating me. Do you want to go through my things to see if you can find any traces of a woman?"

"No, no need for all that. I was just trying to make conversation... unless..." I smile trying to refrain from laughing.

He shakes his head as if to say I was a piece a work. On that note, I allowed my senses to be guide and tamed myself so I could relax and enjoy the moment. After all, we just met, so if he did have someone, I couldn't be mad at him. A brotha as fine as him couldn't help but to be taken. But right now, that wasn't my problem. If he was taken, then his woman should've been here with him.

He walks closer to me, telling me to relax. As I prepare to open my mouth to start talking again, he puts his finger over my lips, gently kisses them and lowers me to his bed. An instant chemistry overcomes the both of us, and we engage in a passionate kiss. His hands caress my inner thigh and then move further up my leg. I let out a moan telling him that I want more, and began caressing his neck with my lips. As the passion gets stronger, he lays on top of me as if he wants me to feel his hardness.

Unable to resists the temptation, curiosity gets the best of me and I start unzipping his pants just as my phone starts to ring.

As I try to ignore the constant refrains of my ringtone, I lean over to silence it, but see that it's a call from the kids and decide to answer it.

"Umm...hello?" I answered, sounding as if I had just awakened.

"Momma, how's your date?" Sasha asked.

"It's going good," I paused while sitting up. "Why are you not in bed? You don't have to wait up for me; you know Aunt Tracy said that ya'll could spend the night with her."

She quickly responds, "The kids are already in bed asleep. I wanted to make sure that you were okay since you hadn't called us yet."

I was *more* than okay, but felt bad for not calling. Although she was still young, I was glad to know that she was mature and caring enough to make sure that her momma was okay.

"I'm fine. Thank you for checking. I'm sorry I haven't called you yet. Now get some rest, you know we're going to Sunday school in the morning." I kindly demanded.

Lord knew that church was one place I definitely needed to be after the thoughts that I had going in my mind.

She interrupts, "Momma?"

"Yes?" I wait for her to finish.

"Never mind, I'll see you in the morning."

I tell her I would see her tonight and then she hands the phone to Tracy.

Enthusiastically like it's midday Tracy asks, "Hey chic, whatcha doin'? Freakin?"

I laugh out loud, and lie "No—I was interrupted! And hey! Don't let Sasha hear you talking like that!"

To her defense, she responds, "Hey don't be getting an attitude with me. You told me to call if you weren't here by now so I could stop you from doing something you would regret later."

I scratch the back of my neck as if I had something on it, and looked at Brian who was lying beside me patiently waiting for me to get off the phone so we could finish getting our freak on and then some.

"Damn, you're right. Good looking out."

We hang up the phone and I immediately call back, asking for Sasha. I knew there was something she wanted to ask me, but for some reason was afraid to ask. If there was any way that I could prevent her from feeling like she did earlier, I was going to try my hardest. I figured that she wanted to ask about the outfit, and although I wanted to surprise her, I didn't want it to be on her mind any longer than it already had been.

"Sasha?" I asked when I heard her voice.

"Yes Momma, I'm going to bed right now!" she quickly answered.

I chuckled.

"What shoes are you going to wear with this outfit I got from Sanaiz Styles?" I smiled.

She started screaming, and I could tell that she was jumping up and down.

"Ooh Momma, thank you so much! I love you sooo much Momma," she excitedly exclaimed. Chills ran up my spine as I told her she was welcome. Before I could say anything else, I heard a dial tone and I hung up.

I turned to Brian who was lying on his back with his arms around the back of his neck as he watched a basketball game.

"I have a feeling that something is going to happen that we both might regret, so I'm going to get up and allow you to take me back to my car."

Without turning away from the game, he asked. "Is that what you want, or are you just trying to be good?"

He knew the answer before I could respond and instead of allowing me to speak, he raised my shirt, unbuttoned my bra and began caressing my nipples before placing them in his mouth.

He teased one and then the other as if the other was getting jealous. From there he went to my navel and kept it company before unbuttoning my jeans. I knew it was time to go, but it felt as if the alcohol had returned to my system and my body went limp.

Before I knew it, I woke up at the sound of the alarm clock.

I jumped up thinking that it was my phone and that Tracy was call-ing to find out where I was.

I thought I overslept and was still at Brian's.

"Damn how did I let this happen?" I thought, trying to scramble out of bed.

I felt like such an idiot.

"I told myself that I was not going to let anything happen between us, and look at me now, he got just what he wanted. I ruined it by giving in and will probably never hear from him again." I cursed myself.

I heard Tracy laughing as she stood at the door. I looked at her, confused.

"Calm down, girl. He brought you here last night. You either had too much to drink or too much sex."

I started to settle down and took a deep breath. "He brought me here last night?"

She told me that Brian called to tell her that I had passed out, and she asked for him to bring me to her house. She helped him bring me in and got me into bed.

"So where's my car?" I asked.

She laughed and told me that it was still at Applebee's where I left it before going to the mall.

I was embarrassed and pissed off at the same time. How dare he sleep with me and then drop me off at someone else's house? I guess he had to get me out before another chic arrived. He had it all planned, and here I was, the desperate fool who fell for it.

I asked Tracy for a favor.

"You mind watching the kids for about 30 minutes? I need to get the kids to Sunday school, but there is something I have to take care of first."

I figured it would be best to do all the cussing I could before church so I wouldn't after I got out. I couldn't believe that I didn't even remem-ber if the sex was good or not.

I called Brian, but he refused to answer. His cell automatically trans-ferred me to voicemail, so I assumed he was screening my calls and refusing to answer because he knew I was onto his game. I called a few more times, and still no answer.

As I hung up the phone, Sasha jumped on the bed. She gave me a hug while planting a kiss on my cheek thanking me for her outfit.

"Thank you again, Momma. Where is it?" she questions.

I tell her that it's in the car and she'll get it as soon as we pick the car up. She asks why the car isn't outside and I quickly lie, saying the car wouldn't start when I wanted to leave. I didn't want her thinking that her momma was some kind of whore.

Sasha stands up to walk out of the room, looking as beautiful as ever. Her hair hung down her back, flowing like the River Jordan. It was jet black and soft as silk. Her olive complexion was glowing because she knew she was going to look as good as her friends were in their outfits. I thought she would ask where I got the money, but I guess it didn't matter. She didn't have to go to school feeling ashamed, and that was all that mattered.

Giving In

As Tracy drove me to Applebees, I could feel myself going into a daze, still shocked that I did what I did to myself. I got upset again when I thought about what Brian had done to me. I got jerked back into the present when the car suddenly comes to a screeching halt. Tracy's cussing out some guy who she almost hits since he stopped at a yellow light. I looked at her with a blank stare and ask.

"Were you not paying attention to where you were going?"

"No," she says with an attitude. She said she was paying attention to me instead, since it looked like I was in another world.

"I'm sorry, girl. Look can you just drop me off and take the kids to church? I got some business that I need to handle. I'll be back at the house by the time ya'll get home from church."

After she dropped me off, I thought about popping up at Brian's place. I figured that if he allowed me to come over, to get a piece of me, he wouldn't mind that I was willing to come over to give him more. But this time it would be a piece of my mind.

I knew the area he lived in, but was unsure of the exact address, so I drove around for awhile until I saw his car parked in between two pickup trucks. I didn't think of it as being a coincidence that his small vehicle was hidden between these two monster trucks.

I noticed his sleek, black Pontiac Solstice sitting there, looking as luxurious as it did the night he came to my place. I had to admit, it was a clean ride.

Instead of trying to remember exactly which apartment he lived in, I thought about slashing his tires or emptying nail polish on his hood. As I decided on what my next move was going to be, my cell phone rings.

"What are you doing, trying to figure out what you're going to do to my car?" he asks.

Trying to change the subject I lied. "No, I was actually on my way to church, but forgot something over here and wanted to…no, never mind that, why are you calling now?" I questioned.

"Didn't you get what you wanted? I mean damn, you wouldn't even answer my calls." I snapped like he was my man.

Interrupting me rudely, he defended himself. "Hey, hey slow down now, why are you coming to me like this? I thought you'd be a little more appreciative of me bringing you back to your girlfriend's house."

Unsure of what to say next, he finished his thought "I know you don't know me like that, but I'm not some dog-ass brother. I wouldn't take advantage of you like that."

Dumbfounded, I asked, "Then, why would you have sex with me when I was obviously intoxicated?"

"What?" he exclaimed. "Look, come on up: 11th floor, 2A." he said and hung up.

As I took the elevator up I could feel the tension inside of me. I was not only furious with him, but extremely nervous. The whole point of me going to his place was to cuss him out for taking advantage of me and then dropping me off. He didn't even have the decency to call me to ask how I was or to tell me what actually happened. Despite how angry I was, I now felt as if I should let him explain himself, and worried that I had overreacted. I was dying to know: what really happened? Did we really have sex or is he telling the truth?

As I put my fist up to knock, the door comes open. I didn't see him as I walked in and asked where he was. I knew he was close because I smelled him.

"Quit playing, I know you opened the door, besides, I smell you," I said nervously.

As I shut the door he jumped out in front of me and grabbed me. I let out a squeal and then began to laugh.

He walked out from around the corner looking as handsome as he did the night we met.

"Oh yea, well what do I smell like?"

He grabs my hand while bringing me closer to him. I close my eyes to take the scent in. There was no way I could stay mad. His body against mine felt good and it took everything in me to keep from tasting his lips.

"Burberry—your favorite, right?"

He chuckled and then led me to his bedroom. I didn't resist.

He laid me on the bed and began taking off my heels and stockings. Slowly he takes one foot and gently massages it going back and forth from the tip of my toes to the sole of my foot. When he finishes with one, he goes to the next and does the same. When finished he crawls up next to me, kisses my ear then the nape of my neck and then lays beside me.

"Let's talk, I know you have plenty to say or you wouldn't be here."

I looked at him and went blank. He was right, I had a lot to say and had even more questions before I arrived, but now it was as if they were stolen from me.

After taking a deep breath, I started in.

"Okay. What did you do to me last night? Get me drunk to get what you wanted, and then send me home?"

"What?" his voice shrieked. "If you're trying to make me out to be some kind of date rapist, baby girl, you got it all wrong. As much as I wanted to be with you, I didn't force you into sleeping with me. We started, the phone rang, and after you hung up, you said you needed to go. I tried to convince you to stay, you agreed, but it was only to lay down for a bit. I respected that, but when I saw that you were really out of it, I called Tracy and then I took you to her place. I guess the liquor got you more comfortable than you expected."

I was mad at myself but felt guilty at the same time for accusing him of doing something he didn't. I leaned over and gave him a kiss on the cheek.

"I'm sorry; I should have been more careful anyway. Forgive me?" I looked up at him like a child waiting for a response.

He stared at me before responding. I wasn't sure of what was he was going to say, but I was ready for it.

"You know…." He pauses. I could feel my stomach tightening up.

"It's like we've know each other longer than what we actually have, and it's cool that we don't have to be uptight with each other. Usually when you first meet or start kicking it with someone, you don't know what you want to say, because you're afraid of their response."

I smile and move closer to him and cut in, "Yeah, but that's not how it is with you men though, it's like ya'll don't get nervous."

He erupts in laughter, sits up and shakes his head. "We just don't show you. We have the same fears that women do; we just learn to hide them."

As he's talking, I catch myself staring inside his mouth. Captivated by his beautiful teeth, I'm amazed at how white and perfect looking they were.

He stops talking as he's noticed that my mind is elsewhere.

"What?" he questions.

"What?" I ask.

"You're staring at my teeth like I have something in them." He replies.

"I'm sorry—I'm just admiring them. They're beautiful." I respond.

He lowers his head and kisses me. The more we kiss, with his tongue massaging mine, the more I melt and sink into his bed. I turn him over and climb on top praying that he lets me take control when all of a sudden he stops and asks,

"What time is church over?"

"About 1 p.m.," I say, and attempt to finish what I started.

"Good. Let's go get a bite to eat. I'm starving."

I lay in bed not knowing what to think and ask him where he's going. He tells me he's going to take a shower to get freshened up, and he'll be right out.

"Get comfortable. There's plenty to drink in the fridge, and the remote's by the bed if you want to watch some T.V. I'll be right out. Make yourself at home,"

What the hell? How in the world is he going to excite me, only to take a shower without asking me if I wanted to join him? I felt like following him into the bathroom, but then assumed that he was getting me back for falling asleep on him last night.

As I reached for the remote, I heard someone at the door. I started to get up to see who it was but changed my mind since we were still brand new.

"Brian!" I yell into the bathroom, he doesn't answer. I try to ignore it and focus on trying to find something on the T.V. Whomever was at the door seemed just as persistent as I was, so again I yelled out hoping he would hear me.

I go to the bathroom door and crack it open only to find him naked and deliciously wet.

"Brian...oops, I am so sorry, I didn't mean to...umm..." I stumble over my words. "There's somebody at the door. I...I didn't want to just open it..." I stutter.

Embarrassed, he turns his back to me with butt exposed. Amazed at how perfect and smooth it looked, I stared for a minute.

"Don't worry about it, if it's important, they'll come back."

He turns around and reaches for my hand and places it on his chest. I try not to look down, but can't resist. He pulls me close and starts removing my clothes. The steam from the shower fogs the mirror, and he turns towards them and begins to write, Jae, can we? I bite my bottom lip and nod for approval.

I start to shiver as if I was cold and he pulls me closer. While beginning to kiss me from head to toe, he pauses and reaches into the cabinet to pull out a condom. Instead of putting it on himself, he hands it to me and waits for me to put it on him.

Immediately after, he takes me inside the shower and drops to his knees. He kisses my inner thighs, and then makes his way up to my soft spot. As I rub his head with my hands, he begins to please me more. After several moans, he stands to his feet allowing me to wrap my leg around his waist.

He gracefully enters me and leans me against the wall. Our encounter becomes more intense and I began begging him to go deeper as if I wanted us to become one.

"Brian…" I moaned as I begged for all of him.

He sucked on my nipples and then rubbed his head into my chest as if he were trying to synchronize his movements. While holding his face in my hands, I start nibbling at his ears.

"Did I do something wrong?" I asked when he backed his head away from me.

"No, you you're doing everything so right," he said as he sat down on the seat that was built into his sauna.

He reached for my hand and cautioned me to join him. While placing me on his lap, I sprawl my legs over his, place my arms around his neck and begin to gently ride him.

As he put his hands on my waist, he starts to lift me up and down as if he's instructing me on the way he likes to be ridden. While moaning, he digs his hands into my thighs, proving that I am doing everything all so right.

When I thought that he was finished I began kissing him gently before getting up. To my surprise, he places me on the seat of the tub and digs his head between my thighs in an attempt to say thank you.

With my legs wide open he takes his tongue and slithers around. The more intense he becomes, the more excited I become, and within moments, my body tenses and shakes uncontrollably. To tame myself, I pierce his back with my fingernails and then realize it's too late. My back begins to arch, I see stars, and my body tingles all over.

"Oh God, I love this…" I moan, as my body starts to relax.

When finished he rubs my back, kisses my shoulders and tells me thank you. I smile, gently kiss his lips in hopes that he is fully satisfied and whisper in his ear,

"The pleasure is all mine. Are you alright?"

He nods and tells me most definitely, and then the phone rings. I stand to turn the water off as he starts to remove his condom. While he grabs his washcloth to clean himself off, he tells me to grab the phone.

Without hesitation I leave the bathroom and walk to the phone with him watching every step that my naked body made. As I answer the phone I turn around to find him drying off.

"Hello?" I answer. Silence is on the other end.

"Hello?" I said for the second time. Shocked at the voice I hear on the opposite end, I start to get sick to my stomach.

"Hello? Hello?" she says.

"Is Brian there?"

Damn, I thought, I knew this was too good to be true. She was nice and didn't immediately get an attitude when she heard my voice, but I knew this female was not just a friend or relative.

"Brian, phone." I said rudely.

As if he didn't notice my tone, he asked me to take a message, and to tell them he was getting out of the shower.

I was caught off guard that he didn't care to know who was on the other end before allowing me to tell them that he was getting out of the shower.

With a devious smile on my face, I informed her. "I'm sorry he's getting out of the shower, is there something I can help you with?"

"Oh," she said, as if her mouth dropped to the floor. "Well…um, can you give him a message?"

I told her I could and that I was ready whenever she was. She said her name was Angie, and Mike wanted him to know that they would be ready around nine o'clock. I felt a little more at ease when I heard the name Mike.

Walking out of the bathroom with just his boxers on and towel around his neck, he asks who it was.

"Angie." I said while waiting for his reaction.

"Okay...and?" he asked with eyebrows raised as if he was waiting for me to finish.

"She said Mike wanted you to know they'd be ready about nine." I finished.

"About damn time." he said.

He apologized for having me answer the phone and then began telling me about this deal that he was waiting on. Mike was his partner, the one who often came by to get away from her, his on- and off-again girlfriend. The three of them had plans to open a club and were supposed to meet there tonight to discuss what they need to do before closing the deal.

"Good for you," I said with envy as I made my way to the bathroom.

I thought about what this would mean. Brian in a club surrounded by women was not going to be good for me. But since there wasn't a damn thing I could do about it, I decided to enjoy the time that I had with him today.

As I looked at myself in the mirror I notice how my hair had frizzed and asked him if I had time to wash it. I had no idea what I was going to tell the kids if they asked why my hair was wet, but hell--I'm grown.

It was getting closer to 1 p.m., and I wanted to make sure I was back at the house so they wouldn't be worried. I tried to hurry and get dressed.

"Jaelynn," he calls.

"Do you want to come with me tonight? I want you to meet Mike and Angie." He asks.

Although I wanted to be with him, I told him that I would have to see what I had going on. Besides, I didn't know what plans Tracy had since she had been a God sent for the last 24 hours.

He told me I was making up excuses but understood, and said that I could meet them some other time, which let me know that he had planned on us being together for awhile.

"I only forgive you because you were a good girl today," he says.

That really annoyed me. "A good girl? Who do you think I am?"

"Hey calm down—I was just messing with you." While catching a glimpse of the look in my eyes, he tries to change the subject. Instead I let him know that it was time for me to go.

As we ride to Applebee's to pick up my car, he occasionally places his hand on my thigh, while his other hand rests on the steering wheel.

While glancing over at me he says, "I really enjoyed this time with you."

Trying to sound nonchalant, I placed my hands on top of his while clenching my legs tight and say, "I did too. I can't wait for the next time."

I smile before leaning towards him to kiss his neck.

As we pulled up next to my car, he stops and stares as if he were hypnotized. He tells me thank you, and then holds my chin in his hand and tells me if I really wanted to, I could have him wherever I wanted him before resting his head on the steering wheel, as if he couldn't believe what he just said.

I get out and head for my car, and he rolls down the window yelling out, "There will definitely be a next time, Jae!"

I turn to say "I know," and head home.

Love Gone Wrong

As weeks passed by, the more time we spent together, the more I felt as though I needed Brian near me. If we weren't at his place, we were at mine. I normally didn't invite men over, but he was a worthy exception to my rule.

The kids were fascinated by him and wanted him around as much as I did. Shaun would often say that he one day hoped he would be their daddy. I honestly thought he was saying that because of the things he had—particularly, the car. They loved for him to chauffeur them around in it, and although they couldn't all ride with us at the same time, they each had their time with him where he was able to spoil them individually.

I often reminded Brian that he did not have to do what he did for them since I didn't want them getting confused about his role in their lives. But before I could finish, he would cut me off, saying, "Jae, I got this. Just let us be!"

Not only did he have them spoiled, but he had me spoiled as well. Whatever I needed, he knew before I even asked. He was my Yin and I was his Yang and everyone who knew us could see it.

The deal he had been waiting for had finally gone through, and he begged me to tag along for moral support. I wouldn't have missed his moment for the world, and therefore called upon Tracy who cancelled her plans so I could fulfill mine.

She rented a movie and bought pizza for the kids promising me that she would make sure they got in bed early.

"Tracy, in case I've never told you, I am so grateful for you. You have been here for me since high school and I love you for that."

She understood me when I didn't understand myself. She stepped in as a mother when I felt as if I couldn't handle all my responsibilities. And, since my relationship with my family was still on the rocks, she was all that I had besides Brian.

"Girl, stop it before we have a sob party. You know I will always be here for you and *all* your damn kids," she joked. "Besides, he was meant for you, so do your thing."

"I guess you're right…it's all just happening so fast. I can't begin to understand why, of all the times I needed someone like him before, why now?" I questioned.

"One word of advice girl: don't question it. When you need to understand why, God will let you know. In the meantime, just let it be and enjoy the ride."

She had a point. From then on, I was determined to follow her advice.

Brian picked me up from Tracy's and we met Mike and Angie at an empty loft on Grand. It was spacious and seemed like it would be a relaxing atmosphere once it was set up. Our area needed a place that would allow people to unwind during the week, and it seemed like this was going to be just what the city needed. They had already done some nice things with our downtown area, so everybody felt that it was time to do even more—but just for us.

While listening to him talk about what he wanted, I thought, "This brotha is as fine, inquisitive and wonderful in the company of others as he is when we're alone—and he's all mine."

I was so deep in thought that I didn't realize that they were finished and Mike was attempting to make conversation with me.

"So what do you do for a living, Ms. Jae?" he asks, giving me his fullest attention.

He catches me off guard and I stumble over my words. Of course I could have told him that I worked in retail, but what kind of money was that compared to what they made?

I act as if something was caught in my throat, and pretend to clear it.

"Right now, I'm actually looking." I said while rubbing the back of my neck. If my complexion had been any lighter, I would have been red as fire from embarrassment.

In just the nick of time, my boo steps in to bail me out.

"You know Mike she was actually telling me that she may be interested in what we've got going on," he said, lifting his glass up as if he was making a toast. Mike and Angie looked at him and then at me as if they were shocked to hear what he said.

"Really? You're sure you can be down with that?" Angie asked, one eyebrow raised.

"I don't know Brian...I thought you were keeping her to yourself. Seems like a good catch on your end, brotha," Mike chimed in.

Brian looks at me, and I'm completely confused.

"I'm sorry, but I think I'm lost. What are you talking about? Did I miss something?" I ask in a defensive tone.

"Just chill for a minute baby girl, I'll explain it to you later," he whispers in my ear, hoping that would contain me for a bit.

Thoughts began racing through my head. I felt like the only one who didn't know what everyone else was talking about, and in fact, I was. Once realizing that the wrong impression was being made of me, to keep from losing it, I stand up and head to the bathroom. Brian tries to follow me, but I push him away and tell him that when I return, he should have the car waiting for me.

Going to the restroom was supposed to give me the chance to walk off some of the anger, but unfortunately when I returned, it was worse.

As I reached the table, I found Brian handing some female a business card with his name and number on it. Trying to avoid an even more embarrassing moment, I attempted to hold my tears in and ignored the fact that Mike and Angie were staring at me.

Without looking back, I head for the door without saying goodbye. Unsure of whether or not he was behind me, I went to the parking lot in search for his car. Filled with rage, I decided that if he hadn't come out to take me home, I would've been determined to hitch one.

"Get in," he said as he pulled up beside me.

Like a child, I obeyed and plopped in the seat.

He tried to make several attempts at conversation, but he quickly saw that I wasn't having it.

"I was not giving my number out, you know. I..."

I cut him off. "Doesn't matter, we're just friends."

I stare out the window with tears forming while refusing to look his way.

He starts again, "I guess you want to know what I meant when I said you may be interested in working with us, huh?"

Still no response.

Of course I wanted to know but I wasn't going to be a fool and find out in the state of mind I was in. I was afraid of hearing what I actually meant to him; afraid of getting the answer to the question I told Tracy I didn't yet know the answer to.

"Just forget about it, Brian. I think we all know what your plan was for me. Just hurry up and take me home." I begged as I stared out the window.

As he pulls up to the house, I jump out of the car as soon as it comes to a stop. I slam the door and head to the house without looking back.

Before deciding to drive off and leave well enough alone, he sits in front of the house before coming to ring the door bell. When he realizes that no one seems to care and is not going to answer, he starts banging at the door.

Startled at the commotion, Tracy comes to the door and asks what was going on.

I stand in the doorway looking as if I was afraid to answer.

"Who the hell is that at the door? The kids are sleeping!" she loudly whispers.

I start laughing to keep from crying.

"It's Brian. Girl, look at you looking like Aunt Jemima. What kind of rag do you have sitting on top of that head?" I ask.

"*Answer the door,* Jae, and don't worry about what I have on my head." She shot back preparing to answer the door.

"No! Don't! Brian is a damn fool, and he's trying to make me think I'm one too!" I sobbed trying to keep her away from the door.

Looking puzzled, she tells me what we both already know.

"Girl, you know as well as I do that you are not a fool. Now, if he isn't smart enough to figure that out, he'll find that out in due time and will come crawling back. They always do when they realize they've messed up a good thing."

"But what if he doesn't?" I plead.

"Then it's on him. But don't get stressed over it. He'll be back. Look, whatever's going on, you two will work it out. Anyway, I got somebody on the phone. I'll see you in the morning," she said, before giving me a hug and creeping back up the stairs.

Ignoring his persistent knocking, I went upstairs and kissed my babies goodnight and decided that the next day was going to be a better one. I went to bed knowing that the man of my dreams may actually only be a man *in* my dreams.

Pimp's Girl

IT HAD been two weeks since I had spoken to Brian, but it felt like two months. The first week, he called constantly, left messages on Tracy's phone as well as mine, and left notes every other day begging me to come and see him.

After he got the message that I was not going to respond, he left well enough alone. I refused to answer or return his calls, although I missed hearing his voice and missed him like crazy.

I tried convincing myself that it was best that I let it go since we had only been together for a month. It wasn't meant to be. I decided that I could let go without further hurt feelings and this would just be a lessoned learned. I had to think about protecting the feelings of my kids, so I then decided that I would never again introduce someone to them so soon.

At first, I didn't understand why I was so angry, but when I thought about how foolish I felt about not knowing what they were talking about, I knew I had a right to be upset since I was the topic of their conversation.

The way that Mike and Angie looked at me let me know something was not right, and Angie clarified it when she asked if I was "sure I could be down" with whatever they were proposing. I immediately thought it was something illegal, like drugs or prostitution, and then thought about how lavish his condo was.

That bastard! My mind filled with anger all over again. I felt so naïve and disrespected.

Tracy claims that I was overreacting and had the nerve to get mad at me for acting the way I was.

"Jayelynn, why don't you just ask him what he meant? You could be jumping to conclusions as usual. I'm telling you girl, you could be on the way to losing a good man if you already haven't."

I stare as if I didn't know her.

"Hello? Earth to Jae?" She waves her hand in front of my face.

"Are you just going to let it go and not call him to find out what he meant?"

"I don't know what I'm going to do" I whine. "I want to call him, but then again I don't. I'm afraid of the truth." I flop on the couch and stare at the ceiling, thinking about the time we made love for the first time.

"Dear God, what do I do? Do I leave it alone or do I call?"

Tracy shouts from the other room "CALL him!"

I could feel the anxiety overcoming me as I try to gather the nerve. The kids are at school and the babysitter for at least another three hours, so I can't use them for excuses. What do I say, how do I say it? Should I give him attitude, or act as if I was sorry for walking out like I did?

I thought about how he was going to respond. Would he answer and talk to me, or would he just look at the caller ID and ignore it, like I had been doing?

I decide to call.

The phone rings four times, and as soon as I decide to hang up, I hear a distant "Hello?" I pause and again start to hang up, but stop when I hear the second hello.

"Hello? Jaelynn? Is that you, baby girl?" he asks.

I feel like melting. I missed his voice, his touch, his smell...I missed him.

"What if it's not?" I answer and question at the same time.

"If it's not, then you have the wrong number. I hope you don't though, because I've missed your voice, your touch, your smell. Should I go on?" he asked.

Smiling, I answer yes. Just not aloud.

"I need you," he says.

I start to melt and feel myself getting warm, wishing he was there with me.

"How you doing?" he asks with a sexy tone.

Trying not to give in, I keep the tone I had in the beginning and tell him that I've been good, but better since I was on the phone with him.

"Good. When can I see you? It seems like it's been forever."

I tell him that I was actually busy and just wanted to call to say hello.

"Maybe tomorrow?" I ask softly.

He tells me he's cool with that, and begs me to keep my promise.

I quickly hang up to stand my ground.

What did I just do? I asked myself. I sit and wait for him to call back, but after a few minutes I realized he wasn't calling. My stomach knots up and I'm unable to get up from the couch. My knees were weak and I felt nauseous.

Although I wanted to, I couldn't give in regardless of how much I felt I needed him.

"Tracy!" I yell out in despair. She doesn't answer.

My body was limp and as much as I tried, I still couldn't get up. As I waited for her to come into the living room, I laid down on the couch and turned the television on to turn my attention elsewhere.

As I flipped through the channels, I came across a talk show that was discussing hoes and their pimps and then realized that what I felt was actually true. Brian is a pimp! How else could he live so lavishly and not work the regular, consistent hours that normal people work? Maybe I shouldn't jump the gun and assume so quickly without asking him directly, but the signs are there, and his friends' reactions put the icing on the cake.

Why did he choose me? There were several other women at that comedy show who stood out more than I did. Maybe I was the only one that looked like the fool he assumed me to be. Or maybe my vulnerability allowed me to accept anything that looked, sounded and felt good, too.

I guess he did to me what had become second nature to him. I had to give it to him, though: I always felt that if any man could get my attention after what I've been through, he had to be damn good.

As I continued in deep thought, I was startled to hear Tracy scurrying down the steps. I sit up trying to see what's going on.

"Girl, what's up? You sound like a herd of elephants coming down the steps?"

She laughs as she's looking like she's about to go on a date herself.

"I'm sorry I scared you. I'm about to go see a friend of mine, and I'm running a little late. I couldn't decide what I wanted to wear. You know, I'm really feeling this one. He's a little different than the other ones..."

She puts her finger up as if she's motioning me to not speak—because she knows where I'm about to go. "And please don't say a word, just let me be me," she smiles.

As she gets closer to the door to leave, she turns around to tell me to loosen and lock up.

"Oh, if I don't talk to you later on, I'll catch up with you tomorrow," she says with a wink. "You've been having your fun, now it's time for me to have mine." The scent of her perfume lingers for a minute and I figured that whomever she's going out with is probably someone new. I haven't smelled that fragrance before.

I decide to leave Tracy's and head home for a minute, since the school's right down the street. As I'm walking out the door, the phone rings. I check the number to see if it's Brian calling back, but I don't recognize the number, so I leave and head home.

I should've known it wasn't going to be him anyway since he wouldn't call me over Tracy's before he called my cell, but I was a hopeless romantic.

As I'm walking out to the car, my cell begins to ring. I try to ignore it, but the ringing was persistent. Again the number was unrecognizable, but I answer it anyway.

"Hello? May I speak with Jaelynn?" a female voice questions.

"Who's calling?" I ask, trying to figure out the voice on the other end.

I wasn't going to give the impression that they were actually talking to me since these days even the collection people try to act as though they know you to catch you off guard.

She starts off with a bit of shakiness in her voice, but then quickly clears it up. "Umm, it's Angie, Brian and Mike's friend from…"

I cut her off. "Yeah, I know who you are. How could I forget? Look. Y'all tried to play me for a fool then, but I'm not having it. If you're calling to try to win me over with some fake ass bullshit story, forget it and find someone else to be your little whore."

From out of nowhere, I get this burst of anger not even thinking about what I wanted to say. I was pissed because as a woman, she should've already known how hard things can be on us anyway. Instead of having my back, I felt like she was with them. Maybe I was angrier that she was there when all this went down, and I was embarrassed and mad that she knew what they were talking about, and I didn't.

How could she have the nerve to call me, and most importantly, why on earth did he give her my number?

When I finally finished she started again.

"I know you're probably wondering why I'm calling. It's kinda awkward, see..." she pauses.

"The other night went so wrong. We were all supposed to hang out and celebrate the closing of this deal. Mike and Brian have been so excited about renovating and bringing something new into the city..."

I interrupted again.

"Yeah, I know about all of that. What pisses me off is that I felt left in the dark about the job he told you I might do. In actuality, I didn't know shit about whatever it was everyone was talking about."

By this point, I was talking to her like I knew her, and decided to catch myself because after all, she was on their side.

"Okay, the purpose of this call is not to start anything that has not been started." She said. "Woman to woman, I'ma be truthful with you—alright?"

With an attitude I tell her she didn't have much time since I was going to hang up the phone to pick up my kids. Then, I sat in the driveway, unprepared for what she was going to tell me.

She tries to start again but does so in a hesitant way,

"Look—if you haven't figured it out already, Brian and Mike's business consists of making money off of women."

I chuckle and then start to laugh almost uncontrollably. When I find that I'm the only one laughing, I stop and wait for her response, but after a couple of seconds without her responding, I suddenly realize that she is very serious.

"Excuse me? So, my assumption was actually right?" I question.

"I don't know what you thought, but if it is what I just told you, then yes."

I try to laugh again but believe that the reason for me wanting to laugh is to keep myself from crying. I had presumed right but I wasn't ready to be right. Before speaking again, I cleared my throat since it felt like I had a frog in it.

"So I guess that's what he wanted me for?" I asked talking aloud while hoping that she would give an answer in return.

She replies "I don't think so; I believe he's really into you. I've known him for awhile, and that's why Mike and I both were shocked at what he said."

I started giving into her.

"You think so? Then why would he bring it up?" I asked, looking for reassurance.

"Who knows why men do the things they do? But on the real, if you ever need some extra cash flow…girl, you could do well."

The *nerve* of this bitch, how the hell can she try to convince me to try selling my ass for money? No matter how appealing extra cash flow sounded, I have kids and morals! "Get it together, Jae," I told myself. "You've gotta go pick up your family."

"Look, I'm sure I can, and very well at that. But it's not me. So ya'll need to try your money making scheme on someone else. Don't call me anymore."

I hang up.

As I head to the school my mind wanders, and I imagine what it would be like making a little extra money here and there. I could get caught up on some things and pay some debts off, then I could stop.

Out of nowhere a car horn almost blasts me out of my seat! Thank God for that driver because had they not been looking out for my safety, I would've rammed into the back of the truck that was sitting in front of me.

In an instant, reality sets back in and I try to forget about the conversation she and I had moments earlier. I had more important things to take care of, like taking care of my kids and allowing them to see the woman that I was. To each his own, but as for me, I wouldn't be one selling her ass for a couple of bucks.

Indecisive Feelings

AFTER COMING home and settling in, the first thing on my mind was to call Brian so I could give him a piece of my mind—but I knew I needed to find something to fix for dinner.

After scouring the cabinets to find something easy to make, I realized it was a lost cause. The only thing we had until payday was a few cans of beans, corn and stewed tomatoes. I looked in the fridge and found that pickings were slim there, too.

In despair, I sat down at the table wanting to cry after everything that has recently happened. As the first tear tried to make its way down my cheek, the phone rings.

"Sasha," I called out. "Can you get the phone, baby?"

After a few rings, I got myself up from the chair and made my way to the living room to see who had called.

To my surprise, Sasha was sitting on the couch already talking on the phone with a wide grin on her face. As I got closer, she turned towards me and told the person on the other end that I had just come in the living room. She handed me the phone.

Trying to whisper, I asked her who it was before taking the receiver. She looked at me and smiled even wider before whispering back,

"Brian."

My heart started pounding and I felt instant butterflies in my stomach. Oh my gosh. What am I going to say and why is he calling now? Game on.

"Hello?" I managed, seductively.

"Hey girl. What's up? Why are you trying to sound all sexy?" Tracy asked. I turned around to find Sasha and she was already gone. I had to laugh because she knew that I was going to react as such when I thought it was Brian.

"Girl, I thought you were him."

She questioned, "Him who? Brian? Did you call him?"

I paused then began telling her the phone call I received from Ms. Angie. She flipped like I imagined she would've and told me that I needed to call him to tell him where he could shove it. She actually seemed more upset than I was, and although I was happy to see that I wasn't taking my emotions too far, I didn't understand why this new information made her as mad as it did me. She seemed to be overreacting.

"Tracy," I began.

"Yeah, Jae. What's up?" she asked.

Before I questioned her emotions, I decided to get off the phone. I didn't want to start anything between us. After all, she was all I had besides my kids, and I wouldn't know what to do without her.

"I gotta go. I have to try to find something to eat for dinner. I'll talk to you later 'kay?" and I quickly hung up the phone.

I go upstairs to joke around with Sasha since she pulled a quick one on me, only to find that she wasn't there. I see Sasha coming out of the bathroom with tears in her eyes. "What happened, baby?" I reach out my arms to comfort her.

As I hugged her, the tears streamed down her face.

"Come on baby, tell me what's wrong? What can I do? Is it the girls at school again?" I hoped she would say no, but I was dead on. Apparently, the girls were teasing her again about the way she was dressed at school today.

"Momma, I know that we don't have money like them, but it hurts my feelings when they always talk about me. They say we're poor. Is that true?" she questions.

Before she allowed me a chance to speak, she lashes out.

"I hate my clothes. I hate being *me*, Momma!" she sobs.

No kid should have to go through this, especially mine. My eyes begin to fill with tears and I started blaming myself for not being able to provide for my babies like other parents could. I reached out to hold her hand, and as I felt the softness of her small helpless palm, the phone starts to ring.

Believing that once again it was Tracy, I ignored it. Besides, I wasn't ready to finish our conversation. Now wasn't the time to be worried about Jaelynn, Brian, or Tracy's reaction to everything. This time was strictly about Sasha. Nothing else had mattered but her.

The phone continues to ring. Sasha looks at me, and then heads to retrieve it before breaking away from the grip I had on her hand. Before I can tell her not to answer, she picks the phone up and answers.

I could tell by the way she looked at me that, this time, it wasn't Tracy. I reached for the phone as she handed it to me.

"Can we talk?" Brian asked.

I couldn't decide if I should talk or hang up.

"Jae it's me. Will you talk to me for a minute? I'd like to explain something to you."

With each word he spoke, it was as if my heart skipped a beat, but when it came time for me to say something to him, I was simply unable to speak. I knew what I wanted to say, but the words wouldn't come out. I had too many other things on my mind.

"I understand that you still may be upset with me, but it's not exactly what you think. Can we talk for a minute, or can you meet me somewhere?"

"Yes," I manage, "I mean… no. Look, now is not the right time. Sasha is going through something. She's really upset and I have to figure out what we're going to do." I said.

He stops me from continuing, "What's wrong with Sasha? I'm on my way."

"No Brian. Not tonight. Really. It's okay. It's the same ol' thing. Some girls from school were on a roll teasing her about the way she dresses. I guess it's been a continuous thing. I'll handle it. We'll be okay."

He sighs, "Alright—well can I talk to you later?" he asks.

"Yeah, that'll be cool. Talk to you later," I said before hanging up the phone.

I go into Sasha's room to check on her and she's asleep, or at least pretending to be. I lean down to kiss her on the forehead and whisper that I love her before going to check on the twins and Shauvon, who were in their rooms watching cartoons.

As I enter the room they look at me as though I'm some intruder who has come to take away the T.V.

"Momma, whatchew want?" asked Shaun.

I smile and sit next to him on the bed.

"Nothing boy. I was just checking on you guys making sure you were okay. That alright with you, big man of the house?" I asked.

He laughed while Shauvon crawled into my lap and planted a big wet one on my cheek. I watched television with them for awhile before realizing that I had not started on dinner (or whatever we planned to call it since we had no food for a real dinner).

As I head back to the kitchen the doorbell rings. Stopping in my tracks, I automatically assume that it's Brian, but see through the peep-hole that it's Tracy.

She begins to knock as I open the door and before saying hello, walks inside with pizza and buffalo wings in her hand.

"Hope you got something to drink, 'cause I forgot it." She hollers out from the kitchen.

"God is so good." I mumble as I look up at the ceiling.

"All the time, girl!" she yells out.

Payday was in a few more days and there was just enough money in the bank to pay the light bill. Since I now knew she had a little ex-tra cash on her, before she left for the night, I was going to make sure I asked to borrow enough to get us by with some food until I was able to do some grocery shopping.

She flops on the couch, turns the television on and yells for the kids to come down to eat pizza. Before she gets her sentence out you could hear feet scrambling down the steps to greet her.

"Hi, Aunt Tracy!" yells Shaunice while Shaun and Shauvon jump on each side of her. They acted as if they hadn't seen her in months. After her few moments of playing with the younger ones, she sits up and asks where Sasha was.

"Sleeping," I tell her.

"So early?" Tracy says, puzzled.

I tell her the story about the kids at school and she gets quiet and lies back down on the couch with the children surrounding her.

"Damn! That pisses me off. Why are kids so cruel?" she asks.

Without saying anything, I get up to go to the kitchen so the kids can't see the hurt that was starting to overcome me again. I try to keep the tears from falling, but I feel as though someone had ripped out my insides. There wasn't anything I could do to change the situation be-cause as much as I wanted to give her what she wanted, I couldn't.

As the tears fell, Tracy enters the kitchen.

"Hey girl. It's gonna be okay, we'll get you together, right where you wanna be." "But how? Look at me. You don't have kids; it's just you,

Tracy. Do you know how hard it is to survive? I not only have a roof to put over my head, but I have those kids to care for, too,." I cried.

I felt as if my life was at the bottom of the barrel.

She stood over me and hugged me as tight as she could while resting her chin on the top of my head.

I didn't want to continue being a cry baby so I attempted to change the subject as the scent of her perfume reminded me of her date.

I smiled and asked, "How was your date?"

She pulls a chair up, looks me in the eye and responds in a serious but matter of fact kind of way.

"It wasn't a date, it was just lunch and it was alright. Enough about me. Now, what happened?" she asks with a look on her face telling me not to lie. I felt as though I didn't want to talk about the Brian situation either so I tried to act as though I didn't know what she was talking about.

"Tell me: how are you feeling about 'trick daddy?' I know you're confused about how to handle Brian, but I'm here to help you sort it out."

She knew me too well, and she was right. My mind had been pulled in so many directions in a short length of time, and frankly, I wasn't sure about my next move.

"Yeah, my mind is wandering. It's not because I don't know what to do, but because I thought I found the one. I thought it was different with him."

I paused once I felt the tears coming on again. When I was sure that I had them under control, I continued on.

"Maybe it wasn't like that for him. He knew what he was doing and knew exactly what he wanted. That's how he lured me in. How could I have been so naïve?"

Just the thought of the whole situation made me nervous and jittery, like I was about to have an anxiety attack. Getting up from the chair, I begin pacing the floor.

"You would've thought that I'd be able to pickup on something just by observing the type of place he had."

Tracy was listening, but her mind elsewhere.

"Tracy! Are you listening to me at all?" I asked, as she continued with a blank stare.

"Yea, I just don't get it—that's why I'm at a loss for words," she finally responded. As she began to finish her thought, Sasha came into the kitchen, gave Tracy a kiss on the cheek, got her pizza and went to the living room.

Tracy and I looked at each other, struggled to put a smile on our faces and continued on.

"So, are you going to call him and tell him how you feel?" she asked.

"Do you think I should? I mean seriously, what difference would it make? It's not like he's going to change his mind about what he wanted from me. He's after one thing and one thing only, and that's making money off of me."

"Tracy," I continue, "it seemed as though you were as mad as I was when I told you about what he did. Why was that?" I asked.

I saw her eyes tearing up and before I knew it, she exploded and started stumping her feet as though she was having a temper tantrum.

"Because...you seemed so happy. I've never seen you as happy with a man than I did when you were with him. I mean I know you two claimed you were just friends, but it was obvious that you more than that. You were enjoying yourself and getting out the way that you were supposed to."

With a smile on my face, I stood and gave her back what she had given me earlier.

"It's gonna be okay, cause I'm gonna be okay." I told her.

Then the doorbell rings.

I go to the door and look out the peep hole with Tracy peering from over my shoulder. I didn't see anyone there, so I turned the porch light in hopes that I could see better since the dark was obscuring my vision.

"No one's here." I told her.

"Are you sure?" she asked continuing to peer over my shoulder.

It was strange that no one was there since we all heard the doorbell. Even the kids got up to see who it was.

I opened the door to see if anything looked strange, and then looked down at my feet. A dozen roses with a card lay on the steps.

As I reached down to pick them up, I noticed a car down the street driving off. I tried to make out the model (was Brian the culprit?), but couldn't see. I headed back inside where everyone was waiting to see what I had in my hands.

"Whoa! Momma, who are those from?" Shaunice asked, excitedly.

I was hoping they were from Brian, but since I hadn't opened the card yet, I wasn't sure and told her just that.

As I started reading the card, a smile formed across my face.

"Let me guess, Brian?"

I peeped up from the card without saying anything and squealed while jumping up and down.

"It is from him ain't it?" Sasha added.

"I hope so, because we like him," she continued.

While trying to keep from blushing I admitted that it was from Brian and headed to my room. How could he make me smile when I just found out that he wanted to use me? It was definitely something about him. His charisma just seemed to trap me.

Regardless of what it was, I knew that I didn't want to be freed and prayed that God would work everything out.

As I lay on my bed, I read the card over and over until I had it memorized: "Forgive me Jae. Please talk to me and let me explain what I meant. I need to see you. Call me! We can go wherever you want.... whenever. I'm in your hands tonight."

Tonight was the key word. I took it to mean that tonight, I was the boss, but after tonight he would again run the show.

Of course I called.

Tracy and I both knew that I needed to meet him. We figured that it would be better to hear from his mouth what we had already assumed. I wanted to give him a chance to clear his name although I already knew the truth, anyway.

I put the twins and Shauvon in bed, and told Sasha to start getting ready for bed as I was headed out the door. I told him that I would rather come by his place to see what he would say, and to my surprise he had no objection. He had no idea how long I had been waiting for this night. I know I had swore that I was going to give him a piece of my mind, but for right now the only piece I had for him was a piece of me with my mind following later.

Giving In

ON MY way over, I try to get my strategy together. Do I kill him with kindness, act like I'm not bothered by what I found out, or do I let him know that he picked the wrong one to try to use?

As I pull into his complex, I tell myself that I'm going to relax and let nature take its course. I assume that whatever happens will happen and that will be the way it is.

Besides, I knew that his reaction would set the stage for mine, just as it always did.

As I'm riding up the elevator, an older distinguished gentleman gets on from the sixth floor. We continue to the eleventh when he turns to me asking if I was going to see Brian. I had been wondering when he was going to say what was on his mind since it seemed as though his eyes had been on me since he stepped on.

The way he had focused on me, it made me wonder if he thought I was one of Brian's whores. I didn't think that I was dressed too provocatively; I just had on my favorite dark blue DKNY jeans, with a black DKNY halter and black heeled sandals. Hell anyway, looking good was part of the plan, but I was only trying to look good for Brian, and no one else.

I started getting nervous when I realized he was going in the same direction that I was, especially since he already had it figured out where I was going.

Again he asks, in a matter of fact way. "Going to see Brian are you?"

"I'm sorry, were you talking to me?" I shot back, as if there was someone else on the elevator that he could've been talking to.

"Yes ma'am. Not trying to be nosey, just making conversation. Have a nice evening." He said as he tipped the front of his hat.

He then stopped at 7A, pulled out his key and went in. I was in awe and thought about turning around to go home, but something told me to continue to Brian's since he was my purpose of coming over in the first place.

Before I knocked on the door, I teased the spikes to my sexy cropped cut. As I held up my fist to knock, the door opened and there he was, standing in front of me looking as though he wanted to grab me and eat me up.

Before entering into the apartment, we both stood there looking at each other as if we were both in a trance. As he goes to grab my hand, my phone rings as if it were telling me to slow down before I even started.

I answer. "I'm good, girl. Thanks for calling. Bye." I hang up, giving him my undivided attention.

I take my finger and put it to his mouth outlining the curves of his lips while feeling the softness of them. My hand opens up to caress his face while his hand is gently caressing my back. As I slowly walked into the apartment, he takes my other hand in his and guides me to the sofa. Trying to keep my composure, I finally tell him without thinking,

"I've missed you."

Surprisingly, he tells me the same.

Without trying to spoil the moment I refrain from asking how his neighbor assumed that I was coming to see him although it was eating me alive to find out. I didn't want to mess the mood up and enjoyed the direction we were headed. I just sat with my man and enjoyed the moment.

"So how have you been, Ms. Lady?" he asked leaning towards me as if he was really interested in what I had to say.

It seemed like he had his lines rehearsed, so I didn't think he deserved the full, unrestrained truth from me, either. I answered in a soft, but convincing, way.

"I've been okay, I suppose. I can't really complain. My kids and I are in good health, and I'm in a good state of mind...I think." I chuckle.

"And I'm trying to make ends meet to the best of my ability."

Worried that I just revealed too much, I attempt to correct myself.

"No, scrap that. I *have* been making them meet," he cuts me off and grabs my hand to kiss it. His lips felt so good. I knew it was too early for me to give in, but the way that he looked, felt, and smelled was just enough reason for me to indulge.

I slowly start to rub my hand across the top of his low cut fade feeling the small natural waves on top of his head. I eventually make my way to the lips I had been longing to kiss. I take my fingers and gently caress them while my lips start to cover my fingers before making contact with his. My tongue rolls across his bottom lip while I softly nibble on it before he pulls away.

Unsure of his response, I lean back as though I were a child who had been scolded and begin making excuses for my behavior. Embarrassed by my actions, I begin rambling out of control.

"Umm, I really didn't mean to do that; I actually just wanted to see what you were going to do…"

He stands, pulling my hand as if he were telling me to follow him.

"Jae, I didn't want you to come over for this. I wanted to talk and explain myself to you."

I was stunned. I sat back down, and was actually interested in hearing the lie that he was about to feed me. With my arms folded and legs crossed, I nod my head in approval giving him permission to continue.

He kneels on the floor in front of me as if he's going to propose and continues. "Yes baby, I must admit, when I first saw you, it was my intention to get you to do what I'm used to having ladies do for me. I mean look at you: you're fine as hell, and I knew you could do wonders for me and the business." He paused and looked down at the ground before looking back up at me.

"Being that I do what I do, I felt I could use my charm to get you hooked. But as time passed by, and we started spending more time together, I knew just by the way you carried yourself, that you were not someone I wanted to do that to. The way that you are with your kids and all, I knew it wasn't cool. I was the one that got hooked, Jae. I'm sorry. Please forgive me."

I wonder if there was any truth as to what he just told me. My heart was telling me that he was sincere, but my mind reminded me that lying is what he was best at. Of course he had to be good at lying to promote himself and his "business."

Afraid of saying the wrong words, I sat speechless and continued to listen to him. After awhile I realized that the only thing that really mattered was how good it would feel to have his sensual lips all over me.

I had turned him on mute and was unable to make out any words that he had been saying. In my mind, the only thing that I could hear was me, saying, "Brian shut up and make love to me!"

After awhile, he picked up on my disinterest.

"Do you hear what I'm saying to you? Are you okay?"

"Yes, I hear you, but what I really want right now is for you touch me Brian. Forget all that shit you were just saying. Didn't you hear me earlier? I missed you, I need you right now, touch me please. I need to feel you, can I please..." I begged as I moved in closer to him hoping that he would change his mind about what I wanted to do.

Looking at me as if he didn't know me, he rises up and says,

"No, because you're about to leave."

The mood instantly changes and he could tell that I was pissed. Seeing him had made me hornier than ever and I thought that he would feel the same once he'd seen me, but I guess I was wrong. Maybe he did care about me, maybe he did have a change of heart, but how?

Why did it take him so long to tell me how he felt? It had been almost a month since we last spoke. You'd figure that if he cared so much about me, he wouldn't have been able to go that long without seeing me, or touching me, either. He must have had other women catering to his needs while I was gone.

As I picked up my purse to leave, I give him a piece of my mind. "You know, you are so fucked up in the head. How are you going to lead me to believe that you want to be in a relationship, only to show me that I was just waiting in line to be one of your nasty ass tricks? You claim that all of a sudden, you have this big change of heart and realize that you want me to be with you, but now, you act like you can't touch me?"

I sat waiting to hear what he had to say, and start crying uncontrollably. I headed for the door as my eyes blurred and my nose began running like a faucet. As I attempted to focus my eyes to get out the door, he stopped me, hovering over me like a giant.

With his body against the back of mine, he tries to comfort me by kissing the back of my neck and placing his hands around my waist. I try to push him away with my elbows since I didn't want him to see how distraught I looked from the front. I knew my make up was shot, and I refused to let him see what he could do to me.

"I'm not letting you leave like this. Come on, let's get you cleaned up, you can't go home and let your kids see you like this."

I turn around with my head down and noticed how well his toes were manicured.

"My kids are sleep, so they won't be awake when I get in."

"Good, so you can stay the night with me, right?" he asked.

This was not in the plan. I was supposed to come by, listen to what he had to say, get a little bit of sex and be on my merry way. How did we end up here? Lord knows that I wanted to stay the night, but then that would be giving in. He is not supposed to know that I would do anything for him.

I tell him like he told me earlier.

"No. Tracy has somewhere to be and I promised her that I would be home shortly. I need to go. I'll talk to you later," I said, heading for the door.

He backs away and picks up the phone before I opened the door.

"Jae," he calls out my name.

I turn around to find out that he has the phone up to his ear.

"How about we call Tracy to see if she still has plans this late at night," he states sarcastically.

She must've picked up the phone because as soon as I realized he had called her, he was asking her how she was. He tells her that we had decided to spend a little more time with each other and wanted to know if she had plans. He became silent for a few seconds and then asked if she could look after the kids until tomorrow morning.

As I listened, my stomach began to knot up and I felt the butterflies coming on. I definitely had not prepared myself to stay the night, and Tracy had to know that if I had, I would've told her before I left.

I nervously waited for the moment that Tracy asked to speak to me— even if it was just to make sure that I was okay.

I try to take the phone but he puts up his pointer finger as if he's telling me to wait. As he sees the frustration on my face, he ends his conversation with her and hands me the phone.

I start off asking how the kids were and then apologized for the inconvenience that Brian was trying to throw at her. While looking at him, I tell her that it was not in the plan for me to spend the night, and that I would be on my way since I knew she had things to do tonight.

"Handle your business girl. Love ya, bye." She says before hanging up.

After hanging up the phone, my mind races as I try to decipher what to do next. He then asks for me to come and watch t.v. while lying next to him.

I head towards the bedroom and sit on the bed beside him as he's lying down flipping through channels. He asks me if there was anything in particular that I wanted to watch, but before I could get the words out, his phone starts to ring. I can tell that he's hesitant in answering it, but after six rings, he gets the point that whomever was on the line didn't plan to give up easily.

After a few seconds of listening to his conversation, I knew it was something about business. I tried to pick up on the specifics, but when he noticed that I was focusing more on his conversation than what was on television, he took the phone into the living room.

I attempted to focus my attention back to the television instead of him, but with him I never knew what was going on. He had the tendency to keep a straight face regardless of the situation at hand. I would always tell him that someone could be dying and if another person were to look at him for confirmation, he or she would think everything was okay because he wouldn't show any emotion.

It had been twenty minutes, and he had not yet come back into the bedroom. I was in a daze and began to tire of waiting for him to return, so again I tuned him out and closed my eyes.

After dozing off, I got up to see where he was, since he hadn't yet returned to the room. I got off the bed and headed to the living room to find him on the couch, off the phone with his eyes closed. Not wanting to bother him, I again make my way to the door, but as I successfully open the door, he speaks out.

"Where you going? Were you not going to tell me goodbye?" he questions while lifting his head from the couch.

I close the door and sit next to him.

"I thought you were sleeping and I didn't want to bother you. I'm just gonna go."

As I lean over him to give him a hug, he does exactly what I had been wanting his ass to do since I stepped foot in his place. He passionately kisses me.

As I start kissing him back, I feel the strain in my back from leaning over and proceed to straddle myself on top of him while finding that I fit perfectly on top.

Before long, our naked bodies touched and grinded as if we were making love. I slowly inched my way towards the piece that I had been yearning for and placed it near my mouth.

I teased him with light blows and kisses until I made him moan. I then placed him inside of my mouth and took him in and out over and over again exactly how he liked it.

The intensity of his moans made me wet between the legs, so I guided his hands between them for him to feel my warmth.

When he noticed that I was pleasuring myself more than he was, he then took over and satisfied me like he knew I wanted him to do. When finished, he came up as if he needed air and began sucking my nipples.

The more erect they became, the wetter I became, and was ready to cum again. I placed his hand between my thighs once more, and as he slowly found his way inside, I took his piece and began pleasing him as if we were in competition to see who did it best.

Our mouths gently touched before our tongues massaged one another. We kissed heavily and passionately until it was time for us to catch a breath.

With sweat pouring from our bodies, we finally allowed for nature to take its course. He pushed his way inside of me like he had never done before and in an instant, I felt a chill go through my body.

I let out a squeal letting him know that I was pleased, and began riding him. Before long, we were enjoying the moment as if we were never going to see each other again.

He turned me over and laid me on my back while he loved me like I had never been loved before, and from out of nowhere, whispered that he loved me.

"Jae" he called out, "I love you. I am so sorry that..." he stopped and continued giving me all that he had.

Our bodies were together like glue, and the more we continued, the more it felt as though we were trying to become one.

His apartment smelled of sex. I knew we had been at it for at least an hour and the way we were going, we could've gone longer if we hadn't been rudely interrupted by the friend from hell.

We didn't realize Mike had stepped in until we heard the door slam. I was the first to jump, but Brian was almost at his peak and acted as though he didn't hear Mike come in.

"Damn, man, you working the hell out this bitch," he says.

As I'm trying to cover myself from the sudden embarrassment that comes our way, Brian moans, "Baby ignore him, come on let me finish," pressing his face further into my breasts.

"Brian, stop! Get off me!" I furiously yell out while attempting to push him off of me.

As he finally gets up, he takes the throw that was lying on top of the couch and covers me with it.

"Didn't mean to interrupt, but damn, I might have to get a piece of that." Mike shouts out, with his eyes wide open and focused on me.

Brian starts to put his boxers on and starts to push Mike away from the couch. "Naw man, it ain't even like that. She's different, she's mine and mine only." He turns to me and apologizes for what just happened. He tells me that he got so caught up in the moment that he didn't give a damn who was watching since I made him feel so good.

Although I was proud to make him feel so good - and it felt good to hear him admit it in front of Mike - I was still embarrassed. I moved passed them both and made my way into the bedroom where I got dressed. I wanted to leave but didn't have the nerve with still Mike out there. I laid on the bed and watched television until he decided to rescue me.

Moments before he enters the room I hear the front door slam harder than it did when Mike entered. I sat up on the bed, trying to read the expression on his face, but as usual, he looked like nothing was wrong. Without looking at me, he heads to the bathroom and turns the shower on.

Confused, I lay back down to watch a late-night rerun of *C.S.I.* He yells out from the bathroom,

"Are you coming or not? I got the water hot for us, so we can relax before going to bed."

I remove my clothes, step into the shower and allow the water to beat down on the body.

"I love you too, baby," I say, while I start to kiss him.

We start to make love once again, hoping for a better finish.

Changes

AFTER OVERCOMING the shock and embarrassment of the best make-up sex I've ever had, I was finally able to let my guard down again and enjoy the time that Brian and I spent together. I felt as if I was on top of the world and that nothing could bring me down. It seemed as though my prayers had been answered. We were spending more quality time together, the kids were at peace and happy, and despite what he did for a living, I was able to accept his way of paying the bills.

Although I didn't agree with it, I did accept his view on what women decided to do with themselves. He convinced me to accept that, if women wanted to give their bodies to men who didn't give a damn about them, then that was their choice, their life, and it had nothing to do with me.

I learned to back off when I needed to, especially when I sensed the change in his tone and demeanor. After all, he was taking care of the business that was helping to take care of me and mine.

Every now and then, I would see and hear a side of him that I never wanted to cross. He could become blunt whenever he needed a job done or if his money was impacted. He loved what he did, and if you couldn't respect him for it, he would make it a point in letting you know that you needed to mind your own business. He was an entrepreneur that worked hard to get where he wanted to be, and it was clear that he was not going to allow anyone to step in his way.

Everyone knew that my name was never to be brought into the conversation like he had made the mistake in doing the first time. It became obvious by how much time we were spending together that I was nothing like the previous women he had in his life.

I showed him how to love and respect me, and in return, he saw a side of me that no one knew existed. He made me his queen and as long as I was his queen, he was definitely my king.

Tracy wasn't convinced that I was the only one in his life, but I expected her to feel the way she did since she didn't really trust men, anyway. She had told me that she was happy that we were spending time together and getting to know more about each other, but encouraged me not to let my guard down.

She agreed that he cared about me and the kids, and that he wouldn't do anything to intentionally hurt us—but also believed that, with the type of business he ran, anything could happen.

I was careful to pay attention to our surroundings at all times. I even purchased a small gun and had it registered in my name. I was determined to protect my family when Brian wasn't around.

One night as I was lying in bed reading a magazine, Brian called with a tone in his voice that I hadn't heard before. I tried to figure it out by keeping him on the phone longer, but it didn't work.

"Hey Jae, I just wanted to call and say goodnight, baby girl. I had a rough day dealing with the club stuff, and I need to relax my mind. I'm gonna go ahead and uh, call it a night." Something didn't sound right.

Whether I liked it or not, he had his mind made up. Now, of course there were times when he had called just to say goodnight and that was fine. But a *real* sista ain't gonna sit on that gut feeling when she knows something is up.

"Baby are you okay?" I asked.

He didn't respond at first, but when I asked again in a demanding way, he shot back in a tone that quickly changed mine.

"Damn girl, can't a brother just be tired? I had a long day, my mind is stressed, and I wanna chill and be left alone. Can you handle that?"

I was at a loss for words, and decided to leave well enough alone. I hung up the phone without saying goodnight and decided to stay in my place.

Normally, I would call Tracy and pour out my feelings so I could get some feedback. But with her, Brian was already skating on thin ice, so I opted to handle this one on my own. Besides, it was nothing like what we had been through before, so I didn't feel it was something to completely stress myself over. Besides, he probably was tired from everything he had on his plate. Trying to start another business, trying to look out for women who put their lives on the line while making money for him, and pleasing someone like me. He did have his hands full, so I gave my baby the benefit of the doubt and decided to let him have a peaceful night to himself.

Anyway, I knew before he went to bed, he would call back and apologize like he always did when he found himself being short with me.

Two and a half hours had passed and I heard nothing from him. Instead of being furious, I began to think that something was really wrong. My mind raced as I tried to figure out what was bothering him since I knew that I hadn't done anything to make him mad.

I decide to call him back to make sure he was okay, while apologizing for coming on too strong.

After the third time of trying to reach him, I started to get nervous. Regardless of how tired he may have been, Brian never slept through a phone call. Something had to have happened or he lied to me and stepped out without wanting me to know.

We were supposed to be close. We promised to share everything with one another, so what made him change now? Or, perhaps the better question is, *who* has made him change?

Instead of beating myself up about it and going crazy in the mind, I do what any woman would do. I hesitantly call Tracy and ask her to watch the kids while I go to check on my man.

Hers or Mine?

My body was tired and different thoughts were racing through my head, but until I found out what was on his mind, I knew I had to keep my senses keen to make it to his complex safely. One of the first cars I saw was his, so I knew he was there since he had a rule about getting into anyone else's car: he only did it when he was drunk, or very sick.

It was a rainy and chilly 40 degrees, and I was cold as hell. I had forgotten my coat since I was in a hurry to catch him in the act.

I ran into his building as if I was being chased by an unknown suspect and took the steps up to the 5th floor so I wouldn't have to wait for the elevator. As I got on the elevator from the 5th to ride up to the 11th floor, I prayed that he wouldn't have any visitors.

As I made my way to his door, I heard yelling coming from inside his apartment. I tried to tell myself that he was on the phone in disagreement with someone in regards to one of his investments, but in the back of my mind, I knew it was more than that.

I crept to the door to hear his conversation and to my surprise, I heard another voice. It was one that I had never heard before and not only had I never heard it, but it was the voice of another woman.

Who could she be and what was she doing there? He had often mentioned that he never brought his whores to his place since that would open a can of worms for him.

They were arguing, but what would they have to argue about if they were not involved? I crept closer to the door. There was no doubt in my mind that she had to have been someone who he had been in a previous relationship with. Or, by the way things were sounding, maybe a current one.

"Brian, how could you do this to me? I trusted you and even gave my heart to you. I thought I was the only one," she cried.

She was pouring her heart out to the man we both loved, begging him to have a change of heart. I was dying to know who she was and how long they had been together. I wondered if she too had been someone he had plans for in the beginning of their relationship.

How did he make time for her when we spent so much time together?

"I'm sorry; it wasn't supposed to happen this way. Who would've thought that we would really start fucking around with one another like this? I can't show your face in public...cause then everyone would know that I was fucking with one of my whores. Baby girl, you know that shit ain't cool."

Did he just call her baby girl?

"Oh, so that's how we deal with this? That's the problem Brian, it's always about you, ain't it?" she hollered.

"Okay, then you tell me: what am I supposed to do? What?" he yelled out.

"So who is she? I knew something had changed, and I figured you were stressed about the club like you said you were. Now I know it's more than that."

As I waited to hear if he was going to mention my name, I stood frozen. I couldn't believe what I was hearing. He had been telling her the same lies that he had been telling me! My gut said all along that it wasn't just the club making him tired, but I didn't want to believe it. Tracy was right.

I instantly became sick to my stomach and felt as if I was going to vomit. I turned to walk away but then noticed that everything became silent. Out of curiosity, I turned back around, and continued listening.

"There is no one that you need to be worried about. I just know that it would be best for us to leave each other alone." he lied.

Out of nowhere, I heard her scream and in an instant I dropped to my knees as if someone had kicked me. I crawled to the door and put my ear against it so I could try to make out what was happening inside.

"Please don't hurt her, Brian," I whispered to myself.

Her scream turned into a seductive moan followed by words that were all too familiar.

"Ooh, that feels so good baby. Yeah—fuck me like that..." she moaned. "Brian, I need you and I know that you want me. This dick feels so damn good, tell me that it's mine..."

My mouth dropped. I couldn't believe what I was hearing. He's fucking the life out of her, and here I am, on my knees listening from outside his door.

A few minutes ago, he told her it's over, and now he's giving her exactly what she wanted. He gave into her like I gave into him. I turn my back to the door and remain sitting like a child who had just been placed in time out.

I wanted to move, but somehow, my legs wouldn't lift me up. As I continued to sit in distress, the same gentleman from apartment 7A comes out of his place. He looks at me as I'm sitting on the floor and without saying a word, shakes his head in disappointment while stepping on the elevator.

I stood to my feet and questioned him.

"You knew, didn't you?" I demanded.

"Excuse me—are you talking to me?" he smirks, giving me a taste of my own medicine. I turned my back to him and sat back down by the door.

Damn, he even knew what I was getting myself into.

"I'm gonna give it to you one last time, then were through," he tells her.

As far as I was concerned, he could give it to her as long as he wanted, because there was no longer a Brian and Jae.

He continues in a deep voice, "Ain't nobody gonna give it to you like Daddy, so you better get all you can right now."

She chuckles, and then starts to yell out as she reaches her climax. Tears roll down my face in disgust and anger.

I started to knock and interrupt the moment they were having, but opted against it since I knew that my feelings wouldn't change, even if I did let him know that I knew. And with that, I stand to my feet and leave to go home, which is where I should have stayed in the first place.

As I try to open the door to the car, the rain begins to pour down even harder, and my body becomes drenched. I jump into the car and turn the heat on high, trying to ignore the chills that are quickly taking over my body.

Everyone on the road seemed to be in a hurry to reach their destinations. One car came close to rear ending me when his car slid from one lane to another. My windshields needed replacing and when I turned them on, they left streaks of dirt that made it almost impossible for me to see.

As I drove around a curve, I heard my phone ring. Without thinking, I struggled to get it without looking at the number and answered it.

"Hello?" I answered.

It was Brian. I started to cuss him out immediately, but decided instead to act as though I knew nothing. I wanted to see where this would lead.

"Hey baby, what's up? Are you asleep?" he innocently questioned.

Hoping he couldn't hear the passing cars, I remained as calm as possible. My moment was going to come soon enough.

Answering softly to make him think that I was actually sleeping, I began.

"Yeah, I was resting….and thinking about you. Do you feel better? You sounded pretty stressed earlier."

Almost an hour earlier to be exact.

"Uh…yeah, I do feel a little better. I wish you were here with me, though. I had a lot on my mind and I needed to unwind a bit."

I could feel my temperature rising and heart palpitating. It was taking everything in me to continue the conversation calmly.

"I had you on my mind and it kept me from going to sleep so I really didn't get to relax like I wanted. Damn Jae, baby, you got me going." He waits for my response, and I couldn't hold back any longer.

"Fuck you, son of a bitch! I'm not for the games Brian. I'm through with you!" I yelled.

I was so angry that it felt like I was floating outside of myself. As I started to finish the other inhumane words I had for him, he interrupted with that professional, Wall Street voice of his.

"Excuse me?"

My pressure began rising, my respirations increased, and I started feeling faint as I mimicked the words he asked.

"Excuse Me? You gotta be fucking kiddin' me Brian. What kind of fool do you play me for? I was there!" I cried.

"I was there when you had that bitch at your place! I heard every-thing. Heard it all. You gave her something that I thought was mine! I hate you. I hate you so much!" I said, trying to hang up the phone.

My energy was so focused on this man who hurt and betrayed me, I didn't see the truck in front of me. The last thing that I heard was a loud horn, and then an explosive crash.

Love on Fire

UNSURE OF whether or not I lost consciousness, I attempted to sit up. Everything was a blur. I saw lights flashing, clouds of smoke, and heard sirens that seemed like they were right beside me.

I was pinned down and thought it was my seatbelt, so I tried to unclick it and remove myself. My hands felt like jelly, though, so I gave up.

The only thing I could see was a person who looked like an officer or paramedic outside the car. His mouth was moving, but I was unable to make out the words he was saying since my ears were ringing. The last thing I remembered was asking him to help me, then, begging God for mercy. Then, everything went black.

I woke up in the hospital with Tracy and the kids surrounding me, staring at me as if I were a specimen they were about to dissect. As I spoke, I noticed how parched my lips were.

"Here's some water, Momma. Your mouth is dry." Sasha said.

As soon as the water hit the back of my throat, I was able to softly ask what happened.

"Why does it feel like someone dug out my insides?"

My entire body ached, and although I could move, I quickly learned that it was in my best interest to lie still.

"You were in an accident after you left Brian's. Your car was totaled." Tracy informed me.

"Am I okay?" I asked in a worried tone.

She couldn't look me in the eye. I knew something was wrong; something bad had to have happened for her not to be able to look me in the eye.

I questioned again. "Tracy...what happened to me?"

She began telling me what the doctor told them.

I had a mild concussion and some fractured ribs. They wanted to keep me for a few days to make sure nothing else surfaced, and get my pain under control. My blood pressure had also been higher than they expected, and since I didn't have a history of high blood pressure, they wanted to stay on top of that as well. They were certain that it was from the pain and trauma I'd suffered, but still wanted to monitor it.

"Well, that's not so bad," I say.

"Yeah," she says as if something else was bothering her.

The kids were getting restless, so Tracy asked Sasha to take them to the vending machine to get some snacks. Knowing that there was more news, I tried to sit up in bed.

"Damn, that hurts."

The IV that they placed in my hand was starting to become red and painful. It looked swollen and I knew that too much movement was going to cause more pain. As I reached for the call button to have my nurse take a look at it, Tracy stopped me and told me that she had something to tell me.

She stared at me in a way that she only stared when I told her I was pregnant. I looked at her with one eyebrow raised and asked, "Why are you looking at me like that? I only get those types of looks when I tell you that I'm pregnant, and Lord knows I'm definitely not."

She sat on the bed, leaned towards me and gave me a kiss on the forehead.

"No, not anymore."

I again tried to sit up before again remembering that I had a painful hand.

"What are you talking about?" I asked, bewildered.

She took a deep breath and then slowly responded.

"Jae...you were about two months pregnant. Dr. David said that you suffered a miscarriage from the impact of the wreck. It was impossible for them to save the baby." She began crying.

"I called Brian..." she continued.

I cut her off. "Don't even go there. I don't want to hear his name even if I'm on my death bed!" I shouted in pain.

I turned my head and looked towards the window trying to hide the tears that were starting to roll down my cheeks. I couldn't believe what I was hearing. How could this have happened? We were always so careful, except for the night that Mike interrupted us.

I was upset that I lost my child, but relieved at the same time. I strongly believed that everything happened for a reason, and there was definitely a reason for this. I knew I couldn't have handled adding another child to my family.

As I turned back around to face her, Brian walks in the room with a dozen of roses in his hand.

He walks towards me with a concerned look on his face.

As he gets closer, Tracy removes herself from my side and heads for the door to look for the kids.

"I'll be back. I'm going to check on the kids. I have my cell phone on, so call me if you need me."

I nod my head in approval, give her quick smile and turn my attention back to the window as if there was something more interesting to look at outside.

"These are for you," he tells me while trying to hand me the vase.

"You can put them on the table."

He leans in to kiss me, and I instantly lean back as if he was infested with something that I was afraid of getting.

"I'm sorry, Jae. I…" he attempts to speak before I put my hand up letting him know that I was not interested in what he had to say.

"There is nothing you can say to me to make me want you here. You let me down, you disappointed me and you broke my heart. Looking at you disgusts me. You can leave now."

I could feel my heart sinking and was hoping that he would leave so I couldn't apologize for what I said. I did mean it, but I didn't want to mean it. He stood up and put his hands to his face then on his waist. He turned away as if he was going to walk out the door, but surprisingly turns back towards me and walks to the bed before kneeling to his knees.

He takes my hands in his and I begin to cringe as if he had some type of communicable disease.

His touch was warm and genuine but I could not give in. I refused to allow him to believe that this was okay. I knew that if I let him get away with this, he'd believe that he could get away with anything.

I removed my hand from his and placed them in my lap.

"I was wrong. Hate me if you want to, but I am not going to let you go through this alone."

He almost sounded if he was about to cry. I look at him as if he was speaking another language, and then sarcastically made him aware that I had Tracy by my side.

"Thank you for being so concerned, but don't worry about me. I have Tracy. Besides, she's not the reason for me losing our child." I said as I turned my head.

"Look, I knew her before we met. We were messing around on and off... I had tried to break it off with her when I realized that I had feelings for you."

I hated him and wanted him to know it. When I spoke to him I had fire in my eyes and hatred in my voice.

"So how long have you slept with your whores?" I inquired.

I spoke before I thought, and realized that I didn't give a damn about what he did.

"Never mind that. No need to answer." I quickly said. "Brian, I trusted you and you betrayed me. What do you think I should do? Say it's okay and allow you to continue disrespecting me? What type of person would allow herself to be treated that way?" I asked.

Before he could answer, my stomach cramped and took my breath away.

I hunched over and tears formed in my eyes. I wretched in pain and he could see the fear in my eyes.

Jumping up, he ran to the door to get a nurse. By the time she arrived, the cramping stopped.

"Unfortunately, this is normal for what you've just experienced," she said. "I'll get you some pain medication and then wait for you to tell me how it works."

"Thank you," I called out to the nurse on her way out the door. Then I looked at Brian. "Brian, you can leave now."

As I lay my head down in an attempt to doze off, he whispers in my ear.

"I'm here for you whether you want me to be or not. You were pregnant with my first child, and I can't forget that, Jae. I'll do whatever you want. I love you. Always." He kissed my ear and quietly walked out of the room.

Waking Anew

I AWAKENED TO the sounds of laughter. The kids were watching *House of Payne*. I didn't want them to know that I was awake because I enjoyed watching them just as they were. It was a blessing just to see their smiling faces. I loved to see them happy.

Each time they turned to see if I had awaken, I'd quickly close my eyes and slower my breathing. I wanted to rest, but was just excited that they were next to me.

"Hey ya'll keep it down," Tracy cautioned. "Remember we're in the hospital and patients are trying to get better. Keep your quiet voices on."

"Why do we have to be quiet when we are in Momma's room?" Shaun asked.

Tracy explained that the hospital was for people when they got sick, and the sick people needed their rest so they could go home and be with their families. He was quiet for a few seconds and then told her that he wasn't going to say anything else.

"Okay, Aunt Tracy. I'm gonna be very quiet so Momma can come home okay?" he whispered.

"Okay baby, thank you," she replied, winking at me.

I could do nothing but smile, and as I did, Shaunice caught a peek and alerted the others. They jumped further up in bed with me, kissing and hugging me.

It was then that I realized Sasha was not in the room with them. I knew I hadn't seen her when I looked around the first time, but I figured she was on the couch to the side of my bed asleep.

"Where's Sasha?" I asked.

"She went with Brian. They went to get us something to eat," Shaunice reported.

As I sat up in bed, Tracy motioned for me to lie back down since she was alright. I did exactly as she said despite how I felt.

"Tracy, I don't care if the kids are starving. You should know that he is the last person I want my child around, and I would appreciate it if you would call him and tell him to bring her back right now!" I demanded.

As quickly as I ordered her, she shot back with a response that I didn't expect from her.

"Wait a minute. You're not being fair! You know I would not put those kids in harm's way. Brian may have made a mistake, but he cares for you and the kids. I know that and so do you despite what he's done."

She takes a look at the kids and decides to leave the conversation alone. In silent agreement with her, I also said no more and started watching television with the kids.

As quietness filled the room a tall, handsome gentleman enters the room. He had a complexion of mocha, soft curly hair with the most adorable chestnut eyes I had ever seen.

"Good afternoon, Ms. Stone. Was I interrupting something?"

"Um, no."

"I'm Dr. David. How are you feeling?" he continued.

I wanted to tell him that I was better since he walked in, but I didn't.

"Could be better," I said while biting my bottom lip.

He looked at me as if we had some sort of connection. I did the same.

There was something unexplainable about this man, and I was going to find out what it was. He seemed confident yet timid; There was something about him that made me want to know more about him, and my goal was to one day find out everything I could.

As I looked at him and then at Tracy, she gave me a look before gently shaking her head no.

"Are you my doctor?" I asked, hoping he'd say yes.

He smiled and made me melt in bed. His teeth shined brighter than the sun that lit up the room while my heart raced erratically.

"I'm sorry, but I'm not. Your primary doctor will be here later on, I just came to check on you since I was the first to see you in the emergency room."

Before I could ask if he could come back to check on me, Tracy chimed in.

"Doctor? Um.." she stumbled.

"David," I said, lifting a brow.

"Right. Dr. David, do you know when she will be discharged?"

"I don't, I'm sorry. When her doctor comes to assess her, he'll let you know. As for you, Ms. Stone, if you need anything, just let the nurses know. Take care and have a good night." He said before shaking my hand and walking out the door.

As he made his way out of the doorway, I tried to make my way out of bed and ignore the pain that was starting to overcome me.

"Excuse me, where are you going?" Tracy asked.

As I was about to answer, Dr. David made his way back into the room.

"I understand that you may be determined, but don't allow your determination get in the way of your safety. Take it easy." He winked before leaving.

I closed my eyes in hopes that I could focus on capturing his scent and then willingly positioned myself back in bed.

"Did you see that Tracy? He winked at me! Did you see that?" I asked with excitement in my voice.

She mumbled, "Yeah, I did, but don't think it meant anything, he probably does that to all of his patients."

"I bet he doesn't do it to the male ones," I mumbled back.

She looked at me and rolled her eyes, trying not to laugh.

Shaunice interrupts. "I saw him, Momma. I think he likes you, and he's cute too."

Situating myself in the bed, I told her thank you and that Aunt Tracy was just jealous. Tracy laughed but then stopped as Brian and Sasha entered the room. Silence filled the room as Sasha walked over to the bed with a Taco Bell sack in one hand and a soda in the other.

"Hey Momma, how you feeling?" She leaned in to give me a kiss.

Trying not to sound as if I was disturbed at Brian's sight, I answered softly. "I'm okay. Are you okay?" I asked, holding her face in my hands. She looked at me as if something was wrong.

"Uh huh. Brian took me to get us something to eat…you hungry?" she questions.

Before I could open my mouth to respond, Brian walked over trying to make conversation.

"I got your favorite, babe. A burrito supreme without onions and red sauce. Extra sour cream," he smiles.

I rolled my eyes and mumbled that I wasn't hungry knowing that I was starving for something other than hospital food. I started to lie and tell him that I was on a restricted diet, but decided not to since the kids were in the room. I didn't want the kids seeing a side of me that they weren't used to and since they were as much in love with him as I was, I decided to show him the respect he didn't deserve.

Tracy felt the tension in the room and decided to take the kids to the waiting room.

"Hey kids, I think Momma and Brian need some time alone. Let's go to the waiting room to eat." She said as she led them out of the room. As they trampled down the hall, I heard them laughing on the way down.

I had to laugh myself while shaking my head.

"They'll be kicking me out of this hospital if they keep this up," I chuckled, before remembering who was in the room with me.

Brian pulled a chair beside me and asked if we could talk. As I stared at him while giving him a look that he had never seen before, he changed his mind and began eating his food.

When finished, he went into the bathroom and turned the water on. I figured that he was just washing his hands, but when it seemed as if it took him forever to come out, I knew it was more than that.

Without looking in my direction, he picked his chair up, placed it at the end of the bed and started watching television. I wanted to ask if he was okay, but was almost afraid to hear what was on his mind.

"Brian..." I began, "I don't mean to be so..." I stopped myself in fear that I was becoming soft.

I reminded myself that he was the enemy and that there was no need for me to feel as though I was the one at fault.

I toughened up and finished, "Thank you for coming. I am tired and need to get some rest. Could you please ask the kids to come back in?"

I positioned myself as though I was going to take another nap and turned my back towards him. Minutes later, he gathered his belongings and slowly walked out the door.

My heart was crushed. I knew in my mind that it was for the best that it was ending this way; however my heart didn't feel the same.

Once the kids and Tracy returned, I perked up for awhile before deciding to be alone and informed them as well that I needed to rest some more.

The next morning I was awakened by Dr. David.

"Good morning. How are you?" he asked.

Slightly embarrassed, I sat up in bed while trying to tame the hair that was obviously all over my head.

"Good morning. What are you doing here?"

"I'm sorry I disappointed you—maybe I should leave," he said.

"No...I uhh...I just figured that Dr. Wilson would be in since he's my primary doctor now. I didn't know you would be back."

"I understand. I'm sorry; I just wanted to come and check on you myself. If that's not okay, I mean...I will understand and can leave."

He was not only handsome as hell, but was painfully shy, and became even cuter when he got nervous.

"I'm sorry; I just assumed that it was against hospital policy for you to have interactions with patients if they aren't the ones you're caring for."

He cleared his throat and this time bit his bottom lip. While running his right hand through his soft hair, he moved closer to the bed and sat down on the edge.

"Yes you're right; however, I don't think I'm doing anything wrong. Besides, I couldn't walk by here without knowing that you were okay. Now what would be wrong is if I just went through your chart without you being my patient." He smiled.

"Well, thank you for coming to check on me. While you're here, can you get a hold of Dr. Wilson so I can find out when I'm going home?" I asked.

As he told me yes, he'd find him, I could see a hint of disappointment. When I told him that I would make sure that I came to see him when I had my follow up appointment, his face seemed to brighten.

Shortly after he left, Dr. Wilson came in to inform me that I'd be discharged that day. Although I was nervous about going home, I was eager to sleep in my own bed.

"Looks like you're ready to go. The nurse will be here to go over your discharge orders and will then remove your I.V. Do you have any questions for me?" He asked.

I didn't; I was ready to go and was growing anxious. The nurse returned with my discharge papers and carefully reviewed them with me.

"You may resume a regular diet, and need to limit your activity for a couple of weeks. If at any time you start to experience nausea and vomiting or a fever greater than 103 degrees, you will need to return to the Emergency Department."

She went over the pain medication that they prescribed and cautioned me to not drink, drive or operate any heavy machinery while taking them.

Before leaving, she removed my IV and provided me with the script for my prescriptions.

"Go ahead and call your ride and let me know when you are ready to be taken downstairs." She informed me.

"Okay. I will. I actually have one last question: I know this is probably none of my business," I hesitated, "but, I was wondering if Dr. David was, umm...involved?"

She laughed. "Yeah, you and everyone else."

"Oh, that figures." I mumbled again realizing that Tracy was right.

"I'm sorry. I didn't mean that he was involved with everyone else. I meant that everyone else wonders the same thing. To my knowledge, he is single. I'll be back okay?" she says as she walks out.

Knowing that he was probably out of my league, I assumed that he was just being a gentleman, and told myself that I needed to get over it and worry about starting my life over again.

After getting everything together to head home, I called Tracy to let her know that I was being discharged. She didn't answer the phone. I knew that she didn't have to work, but I didn't know that she already had plans.

"Jae, I didn't know that they were gonna release you so soon. I was actually planning on coming that way this afternoon, but I'll head that way now."

I felt bad that she had to make so many sacrifices for me, so I encouraged her to continue on with what she was doing.

"No, I'm on my way," she said.

"No, you're not. You've done enough already. I'll call Brian," I told her.

With no one else to turn to, I got my nerves together, said a quick prayer, and called Brian, who in an instant picked up the phone, came to the hospital, and safely drove me home.

Starting Over

ONCE HE brought me home, a feeling of emptiness overcame my soul. As eager as I was to be there, something didn't feel the same. Instead of wanting to be in the comfort of my own bed, I adjusted myself on the couch in front of the television. I was exhausted from what seemed like a long drive home, but refused to allow myself to fall asleep, thinking that the time would come sooner for me to see the kids if I stayed awake.

Brian attempted to get me settled without crossing my path too often. He had put my things away since he knew that I couldn't do it myself. I was weak and helpless and he knew it, but didn't throw it in my face.

I was hungry, but my pride refused for me to ask him to fix me something. I felt that if I had to starve until the kids arrived, I would do so as long as I didn't have to depend on him for anything else.

"What do you want to eat? And don't say you're not hungry," he said with a slight attitude as if he already knew the deal.

"Whatever," I said in the same tone.

I was sure that I didn't have anything suitable to eat, but I didn't tell him that. He could figure it out on his own.

Without saying anything else, he began stirring around in the kitchen. He brought out two waffles, two sausage links on the side, and a glass of orange juice.

He served me like he was my butler and when I was finished, he washed the dishes, cleaned the kitchen and went upstairs to start my bath water.

"Are you ready to get cleaned up?" he asked, standing over me.

My vulnerability was starting to take control—and I was tired of fighting it. I nodded my head and said, "Yes."

As he carried me upstairs, I felt as if I was dreaming. I molded my limp body into his and nestled my head into his shoulders while taking in the natural smells of his body. It was me that he was catering to, and I felt that I now had him in the palms of my hands. I knew he felt responsible for what had happened to me and there was nothing I needed to say to him to make him stay. Whatever I wanted or needed from him, I now had it. I knew that he was going to do whatever he needed to do to make it up to me.

He gently sat me on the bed where I stayed until my bath water was ready. As I waited for him to leave, I closed my eyes trying to visualize the two of us together. Although I knew that I could not be with him sexually, there was nothing that could keep me from thinking about it mentally.

As I relaxed, I felt his warm breath against my neck. My nipples became hard while I became wet between the legs. I wanted him to touch me, but I was afraid. I opened my eyes and attempted to move away, but due to the pain that I was in, my movements were too slow to escape the satisfaction that he wanted to give.

He began unzipping my pants and eased them off slowly while acknowledging the pain that he knew I was in.

"It's okay, Jae, I won't hurt you."

As he removed them from around my ankles, he slowly began kissing my inner thighs. Without putting up a fight, I began rubbing the top of his head while he slowly removed my panties before tasting between my legs.

I let out a satisfied moan, and before long, he was devouring all the juices from the sanction that I had once called his.

The pain that I was experiencing slowly gave way to pleasure, and the climax I longed for was no longer a vision, but clearly a reality.

He slid inside of me as if I was a virgin and began making love to me in the way that only he could. As we embraced each other, I knew in my heart that he was forgiven and I was indeed in love.

I gave him everything that I had in hopes that I could make him forget about who she was. I wanted him to remember that I was the one that he loved, the one he was destined to be with. I was the one who had carried his first child.

I awakened with the kids surrounding me in bed. They were sound asleep, my youngest cuddled in my arms, the twins on opposite sides of me and Sasha at the foot of the bed. Brian was nowhere in sight, and although I wanted to get up to look for him, I was in too much pain.

I lay there for what seemed like hours trying to determine what I was going to do to get rid of the pain. I didn't want to awaken the kids since I didn't want them catering to me. After all I was the adult, and they were still my children.

After several attempts, I pulled myself up from the bed while trying to make it to the dresser that I noticed my pills were on. Halfway there, my legs gave out and I fell to the floor. Proceeding to scoot the rest of the way, anxiety had overtaken me and I could feel the shortness of my breath.

"Calm down, Jae. You're almost there. Don't do this to yourself." I moaned.

I attempted to take deep breaths, but as I began to feel my heart palpitate, I knew that I needed more than just some coaching from myself.

"Sasha." I faintly whispered while becoming nauseated.

As the room started to spin, I noticed that she turned over in bed to face my way. I again called out but in a stronger tone that I prayed my weak voice could handle.

"Sasha baby, please come help Momma," I begged while extending my arm in hopes that she could see me once she awakened.

To my surprise, Shaun peeped over looking off the bed with one eye opened and the other one closed. He rubbed his eyes as if he was trying to make sure he wasn't dreaming. Once he knew that it was real, he jumped off the bed and onto the floor screaming for Sasha to wake up.

"Sasha, Sasha! Get up, hurry! Something's wrong with Momma! What's wrong with Momma?" he demanded.

Sasha bolted off the bed like she was struck by lightning. She fell to the floor with tears in her eyes not knowing what to do.

"Momma, I'm sorry I wasn't looking after you. It's my fault... what do I need to do Momma? Please wake up!" I hear her scream.

"Shaun, call 9-1-1...tell them something's wrong with Momma. Hurry! Hurry!" She demands, crying.

Before arriving at the hospital, I awakened in the ambulance.

Noticing the I.V. in my arm, I assumed that I must have been dehydrated or in shock.

I had felt bad that Sasha had to play the role of the adult during my time of need, but furious that Brian had allowed it to happen. Where was he and why did he leave without telling me?

The first thought that came to mind was that he had some place more important to be, but then I realized that he could have been with her instead of making love to me.

As the paramedics carried me on the gurney into the Emergency Room, my thoughts of Brian soon became a distant memory. I caught a glimpse of Dr. David who seemed as eager to see me as I to see him.

"Back so soon?" he asked. "Couldn't get enough of us, huh?" He stood over me, flashing those beautiful, chestnut eyes.

"Looks that way, but believe me—I'm not here by choice." I said, with a dry mouth.

Before I could finish my thought, Tracy and the kids rushed in.

"Hey Jae, I got her as soon as I could," she panted. I'm sorry that I wasn't there. As soon as I pulled up, Sasha said the ambulance had just taken you."

Sasha chimed in. "Momma, I'm sorry I didn't stay awake to help you. I tried but I was tired."

My heart sank, just as it did when she was upset because she wanted to dress like the other girls in her class. I sat up in bed and attempted to place my arms around her.

"Baby, there was nothing you could have done besides call 9-1-1. Just because I'm not feeling too well right now doesn't mean you have to be my babysitter. I'm your mother, you aren't mine. I don't expect you to take care of me. I just want you to continue being my baby girl, okay?"

She nodded her head in a way that showed me she wasn't really feeling me. Sasha sat down in the chair and drifted off into her own world.

Remembering that Brian was the one I thought I was going to be waking up to while at home, I asked where he was.

"When I brought the kids home from school, he was gone. He left a note stating he would be right back, so I figured once I dropped them off, he would return shortly. I thought wrong." Tracy said.

My mind again raced trying to figure out where he could've gone. He left me alone without even calling to check on me. I thought that when we made love, it was a sign that he was going to stay until I was ready for him to leave. I wanted to ask if he had called to find out where

I was, or if Tracy had called him to see where he was, but I couldn't let them see that I cared.

One of the volunteers brought some games and coloring books for the kids while we were in the E.R. awaiting for a bed upstairs.

Tracy needed to step out to run some last minute errands before visiting hours were over, and said she would be back to get the kids a little later on. As I waited for her to return, I continued to wonder where Brian was. I reached for the phone to call him to see if he had planned on coming back. Just as I started dialing his number, the care assistant entered the room requesting to check my vitals.

"Hi. I'm here to check your temperature and blood pressure," she announced.

I sat up in bed, moving the kids over so she could have room. My temperature was 102.4.

"Why am I running a temperature?" I asked.

She looked at me with a look on her face as if she was unsure and told me that she didn't know, but that she would send the nurse in. As she walked out and closed the curtain for my privacy, I peeked out to see where Dr. David was.

Excitement grew inside of me when I saw the curtain move. Instead of it being him, it was a tall, older looking lady that entered the room. She had a medicine cup in one hand and a chart in the other.

In desperation, I again questioned why I was running a temperature.

"Don't know yet. When your lab results come back we will have a better idea. Could be an infection of some sort. In the meantime we'll keep an eye on you and wait for the cultures to return. The doctor will be in shortly to talk with you. Here—take this Tylenol." She handed them to me with some water and left.

I wanted to ask which doctor would be in to see me, but refrained. I didn't want to make it obvious that I was interested in Dr. David.

There was something about him that I lusted for. I knew that it would be a cold day in hell before I could ever be with someone like him, but I figured I wasn't doing any harm imagining that hell had frozen over.

Later on that evening, Tracy came back for the kids and after they left, I decided to watch some television to keep from falling asleep.

I awakened with Brian holding my hand. Startled, I pulled away from him.

"Lay back down. Everything's cool," he cautioned.

I wanted to tell him that he was a lie since he left me home by myself without letting me know that he was leaving. I guess he knew he was in the wrong because before I opened my mouth to give a piece of my mind he started apologizing, again.

"I'm sorry; I can't explain to you how sorry I am for leaving without waking you. I figured I could make a run and be right back, but something came up."

I rolled my eyes at him before turning away. How could I let him continue to hurt me? I knew that I wasn't the best catch in the world, but I did feel as though I had something to offer, too. Without even being married, I found myself being submissive to him and giving him anything that he wanted. I was a damn good woman, but for him, it never seemed to be enough.

"Jae, I will do anything to make it up to you. I know that had it not been for my stupidity, you wouldn't be here in the first place."

He lays his head on my stomach and grabs my other hand holding them both as tight as he can. I pull one hand from his lifting his head to only see tears in his eyes. I too began to cry and tell him not to worry and that everything would be okay.

Now was not the time for us to be at odds; I needed him, although I tried desperately to deny it. Right now, the only thing that mattered was that he was here with me.

I leaned down to kiss him and as he kissed me back without noticing that the care assistant had entered the room again to recheck my temperature.

"Ahem..." she said as if to clear her throat.

Quickly rising up, Brian apologized and moved out of the way.

Although my temperature was dropping, the nurse had told me that they wanted to watch me through the night. They started me on I.V. antibiotics, and wanted to make sure they were going to help.

"I'll try not to bother you anymore. Just call if you need anything."

"Miss..." I stopped her.

"Would it be okay if he stayed the night?" I questioned.

"I can find out. Since they haven't put you in a floor bed, he may not be able to, but we'll see."

"I'm sorry ma'am, but why haven't they put her up on the floor yet? Why is she still down here in the E.R?" he confusingly asked.

"You know, I don't know. I'll have her doctor come in." She walked out.

Shortly after, Dr. David arrives. I could tell by the way Brian stood to his feet that he was somewhat intimidated.

Without even glancing at Brian, he came straight to my bed to shake my hand. Noticing this, Brian extended his first.

"Hey doc. I'm Brian, her fiancé," he lies.

With a bewildered look on his face, Dr. David forms a smile and tells him that it was a pleasure meeting him.

"What can I do for you, Ms. Stone?" he asks.

Before I could open my mouth to answer, Brian again cuts in.

"Well, I actually called you in. I was wondering why she hasn't made it to the floor yet? It's been a couple of hours since she's been down here."

Dr. David chuckles before answering.

"Yes, I know that. There are times when some patients are more critical than others and with that being so, they are transferred first."

I stare at him in awe, taking in his natural beauty.

"I felt that since she may be ready to go home in the morning, I would have her stay down here to avoid having her go through the different changes."

"That's understandable. Thank you, doctor," I said as I gave him a gentle smile.

"Is there anything else I can do for you?" he asked while looking at the both of us.

I shake my head no and glance at Brian who was obviously upset.

Brian shakes his head no and leaves the room while leaving the two of us together.

"Fiance?" Dr. David asks.

"No. Boyfriend. Actually, ex-boyfriend." I answer.

"Good. I'll be back later to check on you." He leaves the room with a smile on his face.

Jobless

IN THE days following my hospitalization, I could feel my body returning to normal and I finally started believing that the worse was behind me. Although I tried my damndest to follow my discharge instructions and keep my activity to a minimum, I felt helpless and attempted to do what I could to help out.

My discharge instructions stated that I couldn't return to work for another week. I let my supervisor know that, although I couldn't yet, I was more than eager to return. I had to make sure she knew I wasn't taking time off to just relax and get away despite how much I really despised working for nothing. I needed my job.

Because I had no income coming in, Brian practically moved in to help me out financially and in other ways as well. Not only were the kids ecstatic about him being there, but I had to admit, I was, too, since I never knew what it felt like to have someone to help take care of business.

The plan was for his move to be temporary until I was back on my feet. Since we never discussed what that really meant, we played it by ear and never brought it up until our living arrangements became too hard to bear.

We shared our moments and grew closer. The longer he stayed, the closer we became. Despite our recent problems, I was determined to not let anyone take this man from me. Therefore, whatever he needed from me, I gave. I didn't have much to give and he knew that, but he also knew that for him, I was down for whatever.

When we made love, I loved him like there was no tomorrow. Before him, I made a promise to myself that there would be things I would not do with another person unless vows were exchanged. For him, I made sacrifices that disregarded every standard I set for myself. As time went on, I learned that keeping him satisfied was the only way to keep him.

I felt in order for me to keep him fully satisfied, I needed to talk to someone who knew how to get the job done. Therefore, I confided in an old friend from high school who I knew didn't have a problem in keeping any man unless she wanted them gone.

"Hey Angela, it's Jae. How you been?"

"Oh my gosh, girl! What brings you my way?" she asked, laughing aloud. "I ain't heard from you in forever, I'm surprised you kept my number. How long has it been?"

It really hadn't been as long as she made it seem. We had seen each other at the mall about seven months ago, and she tried to lure me into a business that she and a friend started. She said that the money was good and if I ever wanted to try it out, all I had to do was call. Unfortunately, it involved stripping for bachelor parties—and although I thought I still had it going on after four kids, I wasn't bold enough to flaunt it like that.

"This may sound like an unusual request, but look girl, I need your help."

She sounded as if she looked bewildered.

"Girl you're starting to scare me. What's up?" she hesitantly asked.

I told her what I wanted and how I wanted it. I explained my feelings and what I was willing to do to keep this man in my grasp. I even told her that it made me no difference if people thought I was desperate because in reality, I was.

We talked for hours about how to keep the man that you wanted without him owning you. She schooled me like she did in high school, except this time, we were no longer talking high school sex.

Her expertise in pleasing and keeping a man grew as she did. I was confident that the more I followed her lead, the stronger Brian's love for me was going to grow.

I became a different woman to him. I occasionally joked around with him saying that despite what he had seen, I was going to be the only one who made him do things that he would have never considered doing before.

"Jae, you have lost your mind, baby girl. Do you know what all I have seen in my life?"

Without giving me a chance to speak, he spoke up.

"I've seen it all, and quite frankly, you don't have it in you to do what I've seen. Besides, I don't want that. I've fallen in love with you, not her."

I was confused. Who was he talking about? I did not want to start an argument, but I had to find out what he was thinking. After all, I had decided to change my ways in an attempt to keep him from her.

"Who is she?" I stood from the bed.

"Who is who?" he shot back, standing as well.

"You said, 'I've fallen in love with you, not her.' So, who is she?" I asked with eyes wide opened.

He chuckled and wrapped his arms around me.

"'She' is who you are trying to become. Stay who you are—for me, for you and no one else."

He gently kissed my lips and then my neck. As he stood holding me, our breathing became heavier. Since the kids were in bed, we had no reason to be cautious about kids wandering in the room. We proceeded to do what we did best.

I gave him all that I had, even when he could give no more. I had to prove him wrong. I knew he was tired and I was as well, but I decided that, despite his assuredness that he had "seen it all," I was going to make sure that I was his whore in this bedroom.

As our hearts beat erratically, our bodies lay against one another, breathing in unison. My man was worn out, and if I hadn't been afraid of one of us suffering from a heart attack, I would have kept it going.

"Baby, you okay?" I ask with my head lying on his chest.

He let out a sigh before responding.

"*You* okay?" he paused. "Worked you, girl..." He laughed.

"Yeah, you worked me alright, that's why you can't talk in a full sentence, negro," I said, sarcastically.

He wrapped his arms around me as if he was afraid to let go. I did the same and then asked the unthinkable.

"Brian...how good did you think I was?"

"Damn, boo...you were good. I'll be the first to admit...I ain't ever had it done to me like that. Where did all that come from anyway?" he questioned as he looked down at me.

"I don't know," I shrugged.

The time had come for me to ask what I had been thinking about since I spoke with Angela. I told her that I would do whatever it took to keep him completely satisfied and I meant every word I said. I was unsure about how he was going to respond to my gesture, but I had to believe in him as I believed in myself and abilities.

With the accident, it opened my eyes to things that I had not seen before. I thought about what could have happened if I hadn't been as lucky and lived through the accident. What could I have left my kids?

Afraid of telling him what I had done earlier in the day, I decided to tell him now. Besides, how mad could he be after I had just given what he never had before.

"I quit my job today." I cautiously said.

I began holding my breath as if I forgot how to breathe. I had never been as afraid of his response as I was then. Prepared to hold him down from getting up and leaving the room, I got myself ready.

Deep in thought, he laid there. With my head still on his chest, I could feel how differently his breathing patterned changed. It went from being shallow to deep and heavy.

While looking up at him, I had seen him biting his lips as he often did when he tried to refrain from saying the wrong words. Instead of forcing him to speak, I waited.

"Damn, Jae, you blew it," I thought. It had seemed as though he was quiet for at least five minutes.

At last, he responds.

"And you did this, why?"

I knew the reason why, but I wasn't ready to tell him. I had a reason that would be more feasible, but I knew that wouldn't hold him for long either. I decide to tell him that reason anyway.

"I realized that I wasn't doing what I loved. Ever since the accident, I've thought about what I needed to do to be happy for me and the kids…"

He cuts me off.

"And what other job will make you happy?"

I tried to be serious yet sarcastic. "One that pays better."

Silence overcomes him again, but this time not as long.

"Okay, I feel you. So what do you have in mind?" he questions.

I couldn't answer. I wouldn't answer. I changed the subject, and instead of him attempting to force it out of me. He surprised me with his own thoughts.

"Well, I can't be upset with you since I thought of a change as well."

Not only did he catch me off guard, but I was furious and sat up from the comfortable position that we had made for one another.

"You what?" I questioned.

His demeanor remained the same letting me know that he was not moved.

"Yeah, since the accident and the loss of our child, I'm ready to settle and be all that I can for you and the kids," he said with tears in his eyes.

As much as I would have loved to hear this any other time, I was crushed and angry and wanted to tell him how ridiculous he sounded.

"So what are you saying Brian?" I hurtfully asked.

As he rose from the bed, he stood up and knelt on his right knee.

"Jae, you have taught me to become what every other woman wanted me to become. I have learned from you what no one else was willing to teach me. I have found someone who I am equally yoked with and I refuse to lose you." Tears filled his eyes even more.

I was at a loss for words and as much as I wanted to hear what he was telling me, I knew it was now time for him to hear what I wanted to say.

"Brian you know I love you and feel the same, but I don't know what you are exactly trying to say to me…" he again cuts me off.

"I've planned to get my life right. I'm through with what I've been doing. It's time for me to get a real job. Time to become a man." He stood up.

While sitting on the edge of the bed, I patted the bed to the right of me, encouraging him to sit down. I had to put my fears aside and let him know what had been on my mind. The moment became awkward for me as I tried to play in my head what and how I was going to tell him what I needed.

This time tears filled my eyes as I spoke from the heart.

"I need more…not from this relationship, not from you, but from me. I need to feel as though I can take care of my kids without depending so much on you." I paused and thought before continuing on.

He looked at me as if I were a stranger and turned his head away from me.

"Look at me." I begged as I took his chin in my hand. At first he resisted, but then turned to look at me.

"I've decided to work with you, baby. We can be a team. I'm not afraid anymore," I said excitedly as he backed away from me.

"Who are you? What has happened to the woman I fell in love with?" he questioned.

"It's still me. I want to provide, Brian. I want to be self-sufficient, baby. You know how that is. I just want to be happy."

He backed away from me with disgust in his eyes.

"HELL no!" he yelled out.

"Are you out of your damn mind, asking me some bull shit like that?" he shot out.

He stood up and began pacing the floor with his hands on his waist. While watching I again voiced my thoughts.

"Well, what would you do if you were me?" I asked trying to defend myself.

"Look for a real job!" he shouted, ignoring the fact that the kids were asleep. "Jae, are you serious? Do you know how dangerous that can be for you and the kids? Come on, you're better than that."

I tried to reason with him, but the more I tried, the more upset he became. I even tried to convince him that I would quit after a few months; I would save up enough money to get us comfortable since it may take me awhile to find a job making some decent money. I tried to remind him that I didn't know anything other than retail and that finding a better job was going to be difficult in order to support us.

I pulled him close and wrapped my arms around his waist, trying to give him a kiss hoping that he would at least think about it.

While standing tip toed, I softly nibbled on his bottom lip in hopes that he would have a change in heart and whispered in his ear,

"I'll only do it for a little while," I seductively spoke.

At first he didn't seemed moved and pushed me away forgetting the words that he just spoke. After a few seconds, he came back and wrapped his arms around my waist.

"Only for a little while?" he questioned.

"Uh huh," I nodded before giving a smile.

He pulled back from me, gave me a loving stare and in a stern tone, shouted

"NO!"

He had his mind made up and told me that it was time for him to leave for awhile. He said that maybe I would think more clearly if he weren't around and that he too could do some more soul searching for himself.

Before leaving he went outside to warm the car and upon his return, he threw the newspaper beside me on the couch.

"Thought you might want to look through the classifieds. I'm sure there are plenty of jobs that might catch your interest. You should have lots of time on your hands since you quit your job."

Then he left.

I left, too: I left behind the Jae who was afraid of change, and had succumbed to being content with living in hell. I had my mind made up that I was going to provide instead of being the one who depended on everyone else.

Thinking Differently

As MUCH as I wanted to call Brian and apologize for ruining the moment that I had always dreamed of, I knew that if I did, he wouldn't respond.

It had been a week since he had stormed out of the house and I still hadn't told the kids were he was.

"Is he gone, too?" Sasha questioned one day.

She knew how hard it had been for me to find a good man, and now, once I had found one, I let him slip away.

"If it is meant to be, he'll come back," I said, trying not only to convince her, but myself as well.

"What if he doesn't?" she asked.

I had no response for her. At first, that seemed to mature a question for her, but then I realized that she's had to live like a grown up for a very long time now.

The phone rang.

"Hello?" I answered. "Oh hi, Ms. Jones. Yes, I'm better. How are you?" I ask.

Ms. Jones was my landlord. It was rare that she called, but when she did, I knew why.

I had been one of her tenants for years and she knew that unless I really had problems, I almost always paid on time.

"Jae, I know that you've been off since the accident, but I really need to know when you're going to pay this month's rent. I've had a couple of tenants move out, and I haven't found anyone to take over their places yet."

I knew where this was headed, but pretended that I didn't.

"It's put me in a bind, and unfortunately, it's crucial that everyone pays their rent on time this month."

I had to respect where she was coming from. She had a business to run and if I were in her shoes, I'd do the same. She had always been very good to me and the kids and I never wanted to do anything to make her upset with me. Any other landlord would've put us out a long time ago.

Despite appreciating everything that she had done for us, I really didn't have the money to give to her and I told her just that.

"Ms. Jones, I'm sorry, but I lost my job and I am in between jobs right now. I have nothing to give you, but if you give me at least a couple of weeks, I'm sure I can come up with at least half of it."

I knew her patience with me had to be nearing an end.

"I'm sorry, but that will not be acceptable. If you're not able to come up with your rent within the next five days, then…" she pauses before continuing, "I will have to give you a letter of eviction."

My heart felt as though it had stopped. I couldn't believe the words that I was hearing. Not only did I just quit my job, but now I was about to lose my house?

I straightened myself up, cleared my throat and thanked her for giving me a call. She again apologized and told me to have a nice day before politely hanging up the phone.

Feelings of hatred towards her started brewing inside me. Although I knew that she wasn't the reason for this difficult spot in my life, I despised her for what she had to do and felt that it was easier to hate her than it was for me to hate myself.

I paced the living room floor like an addict in search of drugs. My mind raced as I tried to think of ways to come up with the money needed to keep me and my children off the streets.

I knew neither Tracy nor Brian would allow us to be homeless, but at the same time, I thought of all the homeless people who were out on the streets. They probably thought the same thing I did right before their evictions, too.

Many of them had to have known someone who cared for them as much as Brian and Tracy did for us, but when it all boiled down to it, it was probably harder to depend on someone for your living arrangements than for money.

Falling to my knees in despair, I began to cry as if my world was coming to an end.

"What have I done? Oh Lord, I know you can hear me! Please help me! I need you so bad." I begged and cried before God to help us until my eyes were swollen shut. Without being able to do anything else, I laid down in hopes that I could fall asleep until it was time for the kids to come home.

I tossed, turned and constantly thought about how much damage I had already caused my kids. Sasha had grown up being more responsible than she needed to be, while her younger siblings were always aware that it was a struggle for me to give them the necessary things that a mother was supposed to provide.

I slowly picked myself up from the sofa and climbed the steps to my bedroom.

I stared at the bed, reminiscing about the last time Brian and I made love. It was the same night that my life turned upside down.

As I lifted myself up and walked to the dresser, I twisted the cap off the bottle that read Hydrocodone and began pouring the remaining 15 in my hand before putting them in my mouth.

"Jae! What the hell are you doing?" Tracy screamed as she saw what I did.

I jumped in fright and dropped the glass of water I had in my hand. There was nothing I could say. Tasting the bitterness of the pills in my mouth, I spit them out and began gagging.

She ran by my side and started pounding my back as if I was choking.

"Spit them all out…damn you, Jae. Damn you!" she screamed.

With my back hunched over, I thought about what I had done and softly apologized.

"I'm sorry."

She stood me up to face her and looked at me with tears in her eyes. Without saying a word, she grabbed me and held me as if she had already lost me.

She rubbed my hair and then spoke.

"Whatever it is that you need or that you think you need, I will help you get it. Whatever it is that makes you think you are alone…know that you are not. We need you. Don't do this shit again."

I sat down on the bed in hopes that she would follow and told her about the plan that I had brought to Brian.

"I want to be happy. I want my kids to be happy."

"Money doesn't always bring you happiness. It helps, but love is more than that."

She went on to say that since she was not in my shoes she couldn't tell me what to do, but if she were, she would think about things a little more clearly.

"Girl, why don't you leave well enough alone, and enjoy things the way they are? In the meantime, I'll help you find a job—and it won't be whoring," she tried to joke.

The look on my face told her that she was not convincing enough.

She continued, "Alright, don't come crying to me when he's gone. You were mad when you found out that he wanted you to work for him. Now that he has feelings for you and doesn't want you to endanger yourself and the kids, here you are tripping again. Black women...no wonder they go to the other side," she chuckles.

Before I could speak, she stood and started walking toward the bedroom door.

"You betta get it together, girl. Learn to be happy with what you've got and pray that some other bitch don't get him."

She turns around to come back and gives me a hug while planting a kiss on my cheek.

As I try to make sense of what she had to say, I fall to my knees, but this time, pray that God leads me in the right direction.

Sleeping with the Enemy

It seemed like searching the classifieds had become my new part time job. Unfortunately, looking for work didn't pay a dime. I had grown tired of searching for a good fit and was upset that out of the ten jobs that I was interested in, only four of them allowed time for interviews.

Two of the four called back for second interviews but later informed me that they found someone more qualified.

When Tracy noticed that her words of encouragement were now useless, she then attempted to get me on with her at the Post Office. Although she knew they weren't hiring, she went to H.R. to see if she could pull a few strings.

Turns out the only position they had available was for someone who was able to consistently lift 60 lbs. At the time, I had orders not to lift anything greater than 20.

I was getting desperate and knew that I had to do something. The rent would soon be due again and I feared Ms. Jones' call.

As much as I hated to call my sister, I was grateful that she sent me the money via Western Union. It would be a cold day in hell before she'd ever send me more, so I toughened up and made the phone call to Brian in hopes that he would have a change of heart.

He answered on the second ring.

"Yes, Jae?" he answered hurriedly, as if he were still angry.

I was lost, confused and disappointed. I thought that after all this time he would be waiting for my call. I thought about hanging up, but then realized how much I needed him.

"Can we talk?"

"Go ahead."

"No… in person." I hesitated. "Can I come by?" I asked while biting my lip, afraid of hearing his answer.

As I waited for his response, I felt the warmth of my feelings for him take over. My heart began to beat faster and the butterflies that I hadn't felt in awhile came back.

He said that he had to make a run, but that Mike would be there to let me in. When he had mentioned that Mike was going to be there, I was apprehensive. But, since I trusted Brian's instincts and knew that he wouldn't put me in harm's way, I told myself that if he felt it was okay, then it must've been okay.

As I made my way to the door, I found myself straightening my clothing and making sure that each strand of hair was in a place. Before I could raise my hand to knock on the door, Mike opened it as if he were awaiting my arrival.

Without speaking, he made his way back to the recliner I assumed he was sitting in and focused on the game that he was watching.

I slowly made my way to the couch while attempting to make conversation.

"How are you?" I asked in a soft but firm tone.

He gave no response and continued looking as if I hadn't said a word.

I started again, "Brian told me that you would be here, I hope I'm not intruding…"

Cutting me off, he gave me a look that he could only give. He turned his body away from the game and then mumbles the words "You're cool" in a deep and sexy tone, as if he were trying to impress me.

Feeling a bit uneasy, I repositioned myself on the couch and started focusing on the game that I knew nothing about. I started feeling something that I knew wasn't right and thought about leaving to avoid confrontation.

As I occasionally glanced at Mike, I noticed that it was something about him that made him sexy in his own way. His big, muscular physique made him too much of a man for me, but the way that he moved made him a little more appealing.

His bald head and neatly trimmed goatee gave him points, but his smell...Oh my gosh! It knocked him off the charts. This brotha had more cologne than the average department store and when he put it on, it smelled so good it immediately made you wet.

When a commercial came on, he sat up from the recliner and again focused his attention on me.

"I hear my boy has had a change of heart about the business we been runnin'?"

I waited for him to say more. I knew that Mike cherished what they did and I was certainly not going to open my mouth to take blame for fucking up what they had going on.

When I noticed that he was going to wait until I had something to say, I spoke to keep him from staring.

"Well...what can I say?" I began to stutter, like I do when I get uncomfortable.

"I thought that, um..." I stopped, telling myself that I had to calm down before I gave myself away.

"Ya know what? I'm not the one who advised him to do that. He, uh..."

Mike boldly interrupts. "Well, for your sake, you better hope he has a change of heart. What people don't understand is that Brian and I are a one-of-a-kind team in this business."

He stands up as if he is presenting himself to an audience. He begins to talk passionately with his hands about they do. He acted as though he was selling his business to someone who was offering to buy it, depending on his sales pitch.

"Without one or the other, we don't survive. I'm not willing to take that kind of loss," he threatens, standing in front of me.

I again start to feel uneasy and began feeling the moisture between my breasts. As seconds go by, the tension arises in me and I scramble in my purse in hopes that it would relieve me although I had no idea as to what I was searching for.

In an attempt to just call it a night and leave, I pull myself up to head for the door.

As if I didn't know what he was going to do, he places his hand on my shoulder, and prompts me to sit down.

"Brian will be hurt if you left. You've only been here for a few minutes. Sit...enjoy the moment," he sarcastically says.

I obey in fear that it would get out of hand if I didn't. I cross my legs allowing my hands to sit on top of them. My breathing began getting heavier as if I was having an asthma attack. He must have noticed, because he decided to talk in a nicer, more relaxing way.

He mentioned how he appreciated that I allowed Brian to become a part of my kid's life, and that he had started looking at them as if they were his own.

"You seem to fit the bill, Ms. Jae. You take care of your kids like you should despite your struggles. What's even better is that you can take care of my man as well," he comments.

As I listened, I didn't know if I should've been mad that Brian told him so much of our personal life or if I should've been glad that he was man enough to let Mike know how he felt about the kids and me.

Just as I started to let my guard down thinking that everything was going to be cool until Brian returned, he ruins the moment and begins making comments about how good I put it on Brian.

"Yea…you must be damn good to make my boy wanna leave what we worked so hard to build."

"Ya know, it's taking Brian a long time to get back. I think I will call him to see when he will be here." I said as I got up.

In an attempt to block me from leaving, he stands in front of me while taking up my personal space. The more I tried to get pass him, the more he attempted to block me. His breathing becomes heavier and I could feel the heat piercing down on my face. I knew that what was bound to happen in the next few seconds was not going to be pleasant, so I mentally prepared myself for the fight of my life.

"Look just let me leave before something happens that we both may regret." I pleaded.

He gave me a devilish grin and told me that I could leave once he got a piece of the ass that his boy had been hitting. He told me that what was about to happen was not going to be any regrets on his part.

With tears in my eyes and anger in my voice, I pleaded with him until he got tired of me whining.

"Bitch, shut up and take off your clothes!" he demanded while stepping out of his.

As I started removing mine, the phone rang.

He looked at me before walking to get it and answered as if nothing was wrong. His dick stood erect.

"Hey, what's up boy? Yeah she's here, you wanna talk to her?" He handed me the phone with a look that told me he would kill me if I said anything out of the norm.

"Brian, please help me, he's going to rape me! I need you now!" I imagined myself saying.

Instead, I lied, telling him that everything was okay and that I would be here when he got here. I became upset when I realized that if he knew me like he should have, he would've been able to sense the tension in my voice.

"I can't wait to see you baby. Can you hurry up?" I begged, while realizing that I may have asked the wrong question.

Before being able to hear his answer, Mike took the phone from my hand and asked him if he could make a stop for him to get him a 40 ounce.

"Thanks partner. I owe you one." He said before hanging up.

As he went to hang the phone up, he kept his eyes on me to make sure that I continued to do what he told me to.

Like the whore that I felt I was becoming, I did exactly as he said.

Standing nakedly in front of him, he placed a hand on my shoulder easing me to my knees. He placed my hands on his dick and told me to devour it until he told me to stop.

Before placing it in my mouth, I took a breath as if it were going to be my last. While doing what he said, I could feel the erection of my nipples and the contraction of my sanction that belonged to Brian.

Although I knew that I didn't want to be here with him, I could feel that my sanction had a mind of her own and as she became wet, it led me to deep throat him as if he were Brian. In fear that if I didn't do it as if I enjoyed it, I gave him everything I had before realizing that I was starting to enjoy it as much as he was.

His pleasure began making me horny and I longed for the moment that he decided to put his piece in me. I couldn't let him know that I wanted him to take over since he prompted this encounter, so with each moan that he gave, I acted as though I wanted to get away.

As I attempted to rise up from my knees, he pushed me down onto the couch letting me know that he was in control.

A small squeal released itself from my mouth demanding that he let me go. Although in reality, I was chanting the words "give me what you got."

I felt guilty for wanting him since I knew this was wrong. But I believe a part of me longed for the touch of a man since Brian and I had not been together for so long. Maybe I felt as if was getting him back for being with the woman I had caught him with months ago. Besides, who's to say that he wasn't with her while he was making me wait?

Who's to say he hadn't been with her all this time that we hadn't been together?

"Brian can't do you like I can," he panted.

"I'm gonna show you how a real man pleases his bitch."

In my mind I thought about showing him how a real woman pleases her man, but then began thinking of how Angie would feel if she found out that he wanted a piece of what I was about to give.

"Get off of me Mike. This isn't right. Please don't...I'll do whatever you want," I beg as he forces it in.

A sigh of relief escapes from my mouth as the tension uplifts from my body. As he glides in and out of me, I relax and take him in while trying not to give him back what I wanted.

With my hands to the side of me not knowing what to do with them, I place them around his broad shoulders before allowing my hands to caress the baldness of his head.

He felt so damn good that I was unable to resist the moans that were fighting to come from my mouth. I clenched my teeth together in hopes that I could avoid saying the wrong thing, but the passion overwhelmed me and I let it out.

"Damn, Mike...yes...right there!" I moaned.

As best as I could, I tried to resist, but he felt too good. I began fucking him back.

Our bodies began moving in a rhythm. I wrapped my legs around his thighs as if he was Brian while refusing to unleash them. As he pushed deeper inside me, I gave him the part of me he yearned for in hopes that this would not be our last encounter.

Sweat poured from his forehead onto my face, and as I started to lick every place on him that I could, he then tasted me as if I too was his candy.

"It's happening again..." I screamed as I reached another orgasm.

"Yeah I know...let me hear you scream," he demanded.

I moaned, then screamed as I felt the release that I needed. Unable to resist the moment, I kissed him as if he were all mine while giving him more until it was his turn. I clenched my nails into his back while leaving my mark, and as he gave me what I needed while taking what he wanted, he released all that he could while kissing me back.

Disbelief had overcome us both, and without a moment passing by, we jumped up to again get dressed. As we scrambled in confusion, I thought about what would happen if Brian walked in.

"This never happened...I swear I will tell them you raped me."

"If I raped you, then you raped me back. You know you enjoyed it as much as I did," he shot back.

He was right, so right that I couldn't wait for the next time. But, I couldn't tell him that.

"This wasn't what I came here for. It was just alright."

"Well what did you come here for? You knew that he wasn't here, yet in still you waited."

"I waited so I could get the rent I needed. I knew he wasn't going to allow us to get evicted; besides…I had nothing else to do." I nonchalantly said.

"How much is the rent?"

"Five hundred. What, are you giving it to me?"

"I might," he teased.

"Well then, give it here."

He reached in his wallet and pulled out five 100 dollar bills. Waving them in the air, he questioned what I was going to do to earn them.

While walking towards him, I stopped when I reached his personal space. I moved in closer while wrapping my arms around his neck before licking his lips.

"Call me tomorrow and I'll show you." I smiled before taking the money out of his hand.

He stood there as I finished getting dressed, but I didn't have time to stand in awe. Brian was on his way and I didn't want to be there when he returned.

As I walked to the car, tears filled my eyes. I could feel my body shaking uncontrollably and there wasn't any way that I could tame it. As much as I hated to admit it, I had just experienced on the job training with Brian's best friend and unbeknownst to him, I was ready for more. I failed him; I failed myself, but the worst part was…I loved it.

A New Me

BRIAN HAD raised no questions about what happened that night. Before returning home, I had called him to let him know that something came up and I could no longer wait on him. He started telling me that he ran into some old friends of his and in an attempt to catch up on some things, he lost track of time.

He claims that they had a drink or two outside a liquor store and before he knew it, time had slipped by. He went on to say that he knew I was in good company and knew that all was well.

After several attempts, he eventually talked me into allowing him to come over since he missed me as much as I did him. I had no idea as to how I was going to face him, but I knew that I could play it off like I had recently done hours earlier.

"Give me about 30 minutes. I need to put the kids in bed so we can have time to ourselves," I told him.

Although the kids were already in bed, I felt that would give me time to take a hot shower while getting rid of the evidence.

The water beat down on my body as if I deserved the beating for what I had done. I recalled my time with Mike and desperately asked for forgiveness for what I had done although I knew that I wanted him again.

"Jae, get him out of your head," I said to myself. "You know it can't work."

As I attempted to quickly wash off, I heard my cell ring.

Still wet, I jumped out to answer it.

"He's on his way. Can you handle it?" Mike asked.

Smiling from ear to ear, I asked him why he asked such a question. He said that he knew what he was coming for and he wanted to know if I was going to be able give it to him being that he wore me out. He wanted to give me a heads up so that I could make up something now instead of when he arrived. I told him that it was none of his business what went on between Brian and me, but I thanked him for trying to help me out.

Shortly after, the doorbell rang. I became excited since I really wanted to see him so I could wrap my arms around him to tell him just how much I loved him. Yet, although I needed to feel his touch, I was afraid to face him.

How could I look him in the eyes and tell him that I loved him? How could I hold him in my arms when I knew that I would be thinking about Mike and the explosive sex we just engaged in?

He staggered into the house with the smell of beer on his breath. I was disappointed at the fact that he had been drinking and driving, but I was relieved that he had arrived safely. The moment he stepped into the house, he grabbed me and kissed me while trying to remove my clothes.

"Jae, I love you so much. Baby, you know you mean the world to me right?" He questioned as if he suspected that something was wrong.

My mind began to wander as I answered.

"Yes, I know baby." I said as I leaned away from him trying to free myself from the horrid smell that was coming from his breath.

He noticed the distance I was trying to keep and questioned the reason as he lightly swaggered from side to side from the intoxicated state that he was in.

While watching him, a burst of laughter exploded from my mouth and I moved in closer to hug him.

"I love you Brian, but baby you stink."

His eyes were blood shot red and he looked exhausted. Besides the drinking, I knew that something else had been on his mind to make him look this way. His hair had grown out and he was not as neatly trimmed as he had been when we were spending more time with one another.

While holding him in my arms, I questioned what was going on his life.

"I've been thinking, and thinking, and thinking." He said almost in a stupor.

"Did you miss me Brian?" I asked as I kept my eyes on him.

Constantly blinking his eyes, he told me yes before almost falling over.

"How about you come upstairs with me. I'll run you some bath water...to get the stink off."

Getting him upstairs was a struggle since I had to damn near carry him. Although he claimed that he only had a couple of beers, I knew he had more than that.

When we reached my bedroom, he went straight to the bed and collapsed as if he hadn't slept for months.

As he snored, I watched him as if he was my child. He was at peace and because he was there with me, I realized that I was, too.

While he continued to sleep, I removed his clothes and left his t-shirt and boxers on. I felt content taking care of him. As he slept, I promised myself that as long as I had breath in me, I would continue to love him—even when I was with Mike.

I gave Brian the love that he needed while providing for Mike as well. I had no idea that I was going to get myself into the mess that I did, but I felt it was worth it.

When I escaped from Brian, I made my way to Mike in hopes that he could give me what I was missing. Often times he did that and more, although I longed for Brian when the nights became long and tiresome.

While with Mike, I learned new tricks and ways that I could please men to get everything I wanted. Angela had taught me the things I needed to know to keep my man from straying; but he taught me things I needed to know in order to get paid.

I was on a different level with him. I had to be since he was about money and nothing else. When he thought I was ready to move on to bigger and better things, he told me in so many ways that it was time to let me loose.

"Are you ready for the real thing?" he asked as we were lying in bed.

I knew what he meant, but I tried to play as if I didn't.

Looking dumbfounded, I rolled over in bed and asked what he meant.

"What are you talking about, ready for what real thing?" I asked.

"Do you think we were spending all this time together just because it felt good? Baby girl, we got money to make. Your shit is fire. Do you know that I can..." he spoke before I interrupted.

"I don't even wanna know. Why do I have to start now?" I asked, looking into his eyes.

My heart skipped a beat, it was time to move on although I was comfortable with sleeping with just him and getting paid. I knew what to do and what not to do and figured that as longed as I gave it to him like he wanted; he would continue giving me what I needed.

He laughed when he saw the expression on my face.

"Did you actually think we were doing this for the hell of it? I mean yeah you're good, but damn Jae, it's been about the money all along."

I was speechless. Was I falling in love with this man who obviously didn't have any type of respect for women? Or was I in lust since he knew how to take care of me?

"Come on shortie; I know that you are not falling in love. You can't do that in this game. It is what it is. Be ready later on; there are some ladies I want you to meet."

Without a choice, I met who I had to meet, and began my life as the new girl on his list.

He introduced me to some tricks who had been in the game for awhile, and instructed them to take good care of me.

They were his highest paid girls, and the nights that I was with them, our customers received a two-for-one. Our price was $500 an hour, and if he went over or felt that he wasn't satisfied like he expected, we stayed a little while longer while he paid a little better.

They showed me ways to defend myself and most importantly, how to pick up the ones who paid well when Mike didn't pick them out for us.

They briefly spoke on how to stay as safe as possible, while constantly reminding me that everyone knew Mike so it was unlikely that something would happen.

We worked in places that Mike ordered us to work. He often reassured me that there was no chance that I would run into Brian.

"Just chill, he won't be down here. Nor will anyone that knows him."

"Look, we are in it together, but we are some territorial ass niggas. He stays on his turf and I stay on mine."

I looked at him with doubt.

"Whatever, Mike. I'm just letting you know that the minute he finds out, I'm through."

"That's what you think. I own you now. Not him or anyone else. You may be his girl, but you are my bitch. What I say goes…"

I walked away refusing to hear the rest. I then knew that my need for money had gotten me in a place that I had, at one time, refused to go. As much as I wanted to turn back the hands of time and finally listen to the words that Brian and Tracy were preaching about finding a real job, I knew it was now too late.

He hollered out before I got out of site.

"I'll pick you up at eight. Be ready. Time is money."

I heard him and pretended that I didn't. It didn't faze him that I didn't turn around since he knew that I knew better.

We went to a hotel downtown—not a place that I imagined I'd be turning tricks. Mike said that his bitches deserved to make money in the best spots, but he also warned that I shouldn't get used to it if I wasn't giving what he expected me to.

Brian and Tracy never questioned my whereabouts. When they knew I had to work, they made sure they helped me out by finding someone to watch the kids.

As I walked into the lobby, I noticed a man who looked like he was about to tear into the piece of me that he was unworthy of.

Although I knew Mike was nearby, I was still apprehensive.

"I don't know if I'm ready. What if something goes wrong?" I nervously ask.

Mike told me that his customers knew how far to take it and knew what *not* to do if they cherished their lives.

"Do you know who I am and what I would do to him if he messes with one of my girls?" he questioned.

As he introduced me to him, Mike shook his hand, and gave him a look that I didn't see. He told me to do what I do and reminded me that this was the first and last time he was going to formally introduce me to anyone.

He was in his mid 40's and slightly overweight. He smelled good and carried himself well, but in the real world, he wouldn't be my type.

Once we got to the room, he tried to make conversation as if we were friends.

"So what's your name Ms. Lady?" he questioned as if I was really going to tell him.

"Monique."

"That's nice. It fits you. Do you have kids?"

I rolled my eyes as if I couldn't believe what was taking place. Not only did I succumb to the life of a whore, but I was with a man who was a corny as corny could get.

"If I did, I wouldn't tell you. Look, what do you want? I don't have time for small talk." I responded.

We removed our clothes simultaneously and climbed in bed. As I closed my eyes praying that this ordeal would be over soon, he climbed on top of me and took a part of me that I knew I would never get back.

When I got home, Brian was sitting in the driveway. It was later than the time that they assumed I should be home.

I was supposed to be working part time at a printing company in the Fairfax district. I had told them that although it was not exactly what I wanted to do, it paid me more than what retail had done for me. The uniform I changed into prior to going and coming home, was from a friend of Mike's who actually worked where I was supposed to be working.

Instead of questioning the reason of why I was late, he followed me in the house holding the back buckle of my uniform pants.

"Quit pulling my pants, they're already hanging off of me" I whined.

It was obvious that it didn't matter because he continued to tug as if he was in need of something.

"I missed you, come here so I can feel you" he begged.

I missed his company as well, but was too exhausted from the work I had just put in. Despite the fact that I didn't like doing what I had to, I worked the old geezer like he probably hadn't been worked in his entire life.

He moaned and groaned as if he was having an orgasmic episode every two minutes. When I allowed him to be on top, I lay there, staring at the ceiling as if I was bored as hell. I found myself getting mad that I was not at all getting any type of enjoyment although I knew that mine was going to come the moment we were through.

I knew what Brian was wanting as he kissed the nape of my neck, but with each kiss, I squirmed to avoid further contact.

"I need to get in the shower. I've been sweating and feel so...ughh." I said as I pretended like I was shaking something off of me.

He unwillingly let go while allowing me permission to shower.

I guess I had been in the shower longer than I thought, because Brian had to almost beat the door down to get my attention. The bathroom was filled with steam from the hot water that I assumed was going to remove the filth that I exposed myself to. I had scrubbed so hard that my skin felt raw. After the fifth scrub, I figured that whatever else was on me was going to have to stay.

The thought of being with a complete stranger—for the reason I had been—made me feel useless. In order for me to lie next to Brian, I felt I needed to be clean in order to have some type of sanity.

"Jae baby, are you okay?" he asked with concern in his voice, as I stepped out from the shower.

I smiled knowing that the only man that I needed was standing and waiting here at this very moment for me.

He may not have been perfect, but neither was I. I prayed that one day he would find it in his heart to forgive me for the wrong that I'd done. I prayed even more that the hurt that he was bound to feel eventually would disappear so he could learn to love me for the person that I really was.

As I walked out of the bathroom, the towel that I had wrapped around me exposed my wet and bare skin of my shoulders and legs. Turning him on like it had always done, he stared at me with a look of love as if he hadn't seen me in months.

"What's different about you?" he asks.

In an instant, I become nervous as if he somehow knew.

Hesitant, I question him back. "What do you mean?"

While taking my hand, he leads me to the bed after picking up the body butter I had lying on the dresser. As he removed my towel, he gave me gentle kisses starting with my neck and ending close to my breast. I felt as though I had the energy to love him until daybreak, but just as I prepared my body and mind to do so, he surprised me with a different frame of mind.

"When I get finished, I just want to lie next to you. I want to smell you and hold you like I used to do before," he whispered.

I was shocked at the response, but delighted to do even that with him. After applying the body butter to my bare, wet skin, he followed it with the scent of his favorite perfume. It had the scent of sandalwood and jasmine, and although I didn't care for it, I bought it because I knew he did.

I wore it only for him and only when we went out. But since I felt ashamed of my betrayal to him, I felt he deserved it this night, and I allowed him to put it on me even if it was only for him to smell me as we cuddled in the sheets.

We reminisced about moments we shared, both good and bad only to agree that we came through the test of time. Although our road had been a rocky one, he was determined that we were going to have plenty more years to reminisce about.

I kept quiet and enjoyed the moment while we had it. I was happy and content, and was determined to take advantage of it.

I thought about how things could be if it wasn't for my greed. No one would've ever imagined how upside down my life was going to turn just because of money. Brian would've never imagined that I'd betray him for his best friend when I knew that I could depend on him for whatever I needed.

Although difficult, I put my thoughts aside and again took advantage of the moment we shared. I moved in closer to him and placed my hands in his before whispering the words I felt he needed to hear before falling asleep.

"I love you more than words can say and even more than my actions can show."

He looked at me with a starry gaze, drew me closer into his arms and mimicked the same. "I love you more than words can say and even more than my actions can show."

We both fell asleep and took in the happiness and love that the moment had given us. Nothing else mattered but the love that we shared. I prayed to God that he would remember this as I continued to live the life that poverty had forced me into.

Desperate Measures

AFTER MY night with Brian, I knew that what I had started was wrong. I also knew that if I continued doing what I knew he was against, I would lose him once he found out.

I was setting myself up for failure when it came to keeping him in our lives, but at the same time, I was providing a better life for my kids. I felt proud of myself, but continued to feel guilty each time I had encounters with different men.

I thought about how I finally found something that had allowed me to take care of business they way I had always wanted. Although the sane would not relate to prostitution as being a job, it was for me since I was able to be where I often dreamed of being. The hours weren't what I expected, but it all worked out since Tracy agreed to keep the kids for me two days a week. She told me that if I promised to be home on time, we would have no problem. It finally felt as if I was keeping my head was above water. I wasn't as broke as I had been, and every now and then, I took the kids to the movies or out to eat. I even managed to keep a stash here and there to make sure we were kept comfortable when business was slow.

I finally got a chance to repay my debt to my family, and would often hear them bragging to their friends that I was now the "money maker" in the family. I felt it was my turn to give back to them—and was happy to give them whatever they needed if they were ever in a bind.

I'm sure they didn't understand how I went from being poverty-stricken to affluent with the type of job I had (factory work was my official story), but they didn't raise questions about anything, and whenever the word employment came up, I either left the room or discreetly changed the subject. In their eyes, this job was the best thing that ever happened to me. In my eyes, Brian and Mike were the cause of some of the best things that ever happened to me, of course to a certain degree.

Unfortunately with guilt in my mind, I thought about what I needed to tell Mike in order to get out of the wrong that inside I knew I was doing. The words that I wanted to tell Mike replayed in my head like an Easter Sunday speech, but fear often got the best of me when I decided to tell him that I wanted out.

I questioned why I was so afraid to save myself from a life of doom. Most importantly, why did I allow such a man to have a hold on my life?

I was playing with fire, and knew it. The night that I had no energy for my kids, was the night I had my mind made up that I was going to break the news to Mike.

I had it all figured out and was sure that he would understand where I was coming from. After all, we had become closer than close, and despite his macho ways, I knew he respected me.

It was "our" night. I felt that the best time would be when we were in the moment, so as we finished, I told him.

"Are you out of your fucking mind, bitch?" he snarled.

Without letting me get a word in, he continued.

"You are mine until I say you can leave. I don't give a damn what YOU want! I own you and don't you ever forget that. You hear me, Jae?" he persisted, pointing his finger in my face.

I was terrified and didn't know whether to move or stay still. Even afraid of taking a breath, I held it until I knew it was okay to breathe.

Why did I think he would be okay with the decision I had come up with? I knew he felt that he owned me, yet I still wanted to believe that I owned myself. Some of the girls that I worked with told me that the only way out was to kill or be killed.

Days turned into weeks and weeks turned into months. It had been seven months since I had told Mike that I wanted out, and since then, his attitude towards me had changed drastically. He was no longer lenient and had me fucking every Tom, Dick and Harry.

In the beginning, he sometimes allowed me to have a say in who I wanted to be with, especially if they requested being with me. Now, it didn't matter.

"Go to work, bitch," he'd say. When there weren't customers requesting me (which was not too often), he'd send me down to a certain area where the cheapest men around would wander and request me. I then did whatever I had to, regardless of how I felt.

I had my so called regulars and was starting to feel comfortable with them since I knew what they liked and how they liked it. I felt they respected me to a certain extent since we made each other's acquaintance a few times a month. We'd sit and talk for awhile if they had time to chill, and then I'd do what they needed me to do.

Sometimes I'd make it my point to really please them once they opened up to me about issues at home. For the ones that happened to be married, I took to them in a different way and felt sorry for them. I felt that it had to be hell being married and needing to go elsewhere for pleasure or gratification.

On a good night, I would make about $1500 while giving Mike a $1000 of my hard earned money. As much as I wanted to, I dared not ask for more. There were times when I knew I could be bold without getting hit in the mouth, but when it came to his money, I knew when to keep my mouth shut. It was called learning to stay in your place without overstepping your boundaries. I kept my mouth closed until he told me to open when he wanted to get some head.

There were times when he'd say he was proud of me, or that I had been a good girl. And on those days, I felt that there was somehow a light at the end of that dark tunnel that I had been so used to being in.

The night when I decided that it was going to come to an end despite what he had threatened to do, was the night that I met Derrick. Although he was one of the better ones that Mike had brought my way, there was something about him that I was leery of.

Unlike the others, he didn't allow me to make small talk when I tried.

"What do you do for a living Mr. Derrick?" I questioned in a seductive tone.

No answer. He continued removing his clothes as if he was in a hurry. As he took off his shirt, I noticed how good he looked when he flexed his arms. He had the word sensual tattooed on his biceps and I immediately knew that it was going to be a place that I kissed before making my way up to his neck.

I was determined that this night was going to be a good one for me, so I prepared to satisfy him like I had no other. I wanted this one to keep coming back for more and knew what I had to do in order to do just that.

He was sexy; the sexiest one I had ever done. His chocolate skin glistened as he moved and his six packs made him all the more delectable. His face hairless and looked as smooth as a baby's bottom. The more that I stared at him, I had realized that he had Brian beat.

Stepping back into reality and catching myself, I remembered that my Brian was on a different level than all the men I had encounters with. As much as I tried; there was no comparison to him and them.

I tried again to make small talk, but instead of him giving me the silent treatment, he spoke in a way that made me wish he would've continued being silent.

"Damn, bitch! Do you ever shut up? I didn't come here for this. I came here for some head and to get laid. If I want to talk, I can go home to my bitch there."

Chills ran through my body and I then knew that what I did with some others, I couldn't do with him.

Before removing my clothes, I went to turn off the light as I did with my normal routine before I went to work. Again, he proved that he was different and demanded me to keep it on.

"Look, I'm not trying to be romantic either. I want to see everything. I don't know you. You think I'm stupid enough to let you turn off the lights so you can get me for what I got? I know how you bitches work." I didn't respond.

I walked over to the bed with the intent of taking off his clothes to help him calm down.

As I unzipped his pants, I looked him in the eye letting him know that I wasn't afraid of him, despite the attitude he was giving.

Once unzipped, I fell to my knees in order to remove them from around his ankles.

While occasionally looking up at him, I gave a piercing look into his eyes preparing him for what was about to happen. I had never been treated this way and because of the drama that he was giving already, I wanted to prove to him that I was the running this show and not him.

With him naked and sitting on the edge of the bed, I then began removing mine allowing him to see every exposed part of me. As he watched, I teased and stepped out of what I had on in the most seductive way possible in hopes that I could make him show me how eager he was to touch me.

"Get over here, you're taking too long," he demanded as he pulled my arm.

Feeling as if it was about to snap in two, I begged for him to be more gentle since I was there to do as he wanted.

"Ouch! That hurt. You don't have to be so rough. Besides, ain't nobody in a hurry, we got all night."

After damn near throwing me on the bed, he towered over me while I lay on my back. He placed his arms on the headboard and proceeded to put his piece in my mouth letting me know that he was in control.

In order to keep from gagging at how forceful he was shoving it in, I made attempts to get up, but like I fearfully imagined, it was no use, and I continued to take what he was feeding me.

After finally getting off like he wanted, he turned me over to hit it from the back and placed my arms above my head. He held them together and clasped my wrist in his hands as if I was handcuffed. I knew that even if I attempted to fight, he would win, but before he again took what he wanted, I opened my mouth and begged him to stop.

"Derrick, please stop. Could you please get a condom?" I whined.

Laughing as if I told a joke, he continued.

It was like he was an animal and I was his prey. I felt dead inside, closing my eyes in an attempt to leave the dismantled body I was in. I prayed it would be over as quickly as it began.

"Turn over, bitch. I wanna see how good this pussy is that Mike keeps talking about." He growled.

"Please let me go. It's not supposed to be this way. I have kids…"

Before I could finish, he spread my legs apart as if I was if I were modeling for *Playboy*, and began touching me in a way that no one ever had. He was forceful and disrespectful as he dug into me.

As I cried, he dug deeper with his body lying on top of mine and when finished jacked himself off as if I wasn't there.

In a helpless state, I cried out to Brian while asking for forgiveness and try to toughen up thinking that if I didn't seem so vulnerable, he wouldn't have treated me this way.

The night turns into hell while the animal turns into a savage beast.

He repeatedly raped me as if I was trash. It seemed like the more that he came, the more energy he gained. While tearing me into shreds, he calls out a name that I assumed was his girl. But the more he went on, I realized it wasn't her.

"Look what you're making me do. I loved you and if you would have stayed instead of running off with him, it would've been us together."

"Look at me, when I'm talking to you!" He demanded as he held my face in his hands.

He peered down at me as if he was crazed. Sweat poured from his face and onto mine and doing as I was told, I looked at him as I was instructed.

He leaned in to kiss me as he continued to fill me up. I attempt to squirm to break loose, but realized the more that I fought the more he held me down.

I kick my legs forcefully until they become tired, but at this point in my struggle, exhaustion sets in and I give up.

With both hands above my head again, and wrists clasped together with his left hand, he continues to glide in and out with his monstrous piece inside of me.

I let out a scream upon his continuous entering and began to cry as I plead for him to stop. It felt as though he was ripping me apart, and the more I pleaded, the harder he pounded on top of me. My gut was torn to pieces and I knew that I was damaged. He was sweating as if he was running a marathon.

Each time I thought he was nearing another orgasm, he'd slow down to let it pass so he could continue on.

Helpless, I lay there, taking in all that he gave until he became tired.

The brutality that I endured had finally come to an end. After three grueling hours, he finished getting what he paid for.

When finished, he casually dressed himself as I lied mangled in the bed. Unable to move in fear that he was capable of finishing me off, I closed my eyes and prayed for God to protect me.

I had promised that if he got me out of the room safely, this would be the last time I stepped foot in a hotel room with another stranger again.

"Are you going to get dressed?" he asked, as if everything was okay.

I wanted to ignore him, but was afraid of what his response would be.

"I will." I softly spoke trying to stay calm.

"When?" he asked.

"Damn," I thought. "Couldn't he just leave me be?" He rapes me as if he hadn't been with anybody in years, and then has the nerve to make small talk.

I knew I had to answer and quickly if I wanted to escape without further harm being done.

I decided to say whatever came to mind.

"When you leave." I whispered.

Walking to the bed, he sits to the side of me and leans to whisper in my ear.

"Leave now, and remember—it wasn't rape. There were many people who saw you come up here with me...willingly." He says as he walks out the door.

Unlike any other time, I forget about asking for the money.

I lie back on the bed, trying to cry myself to sleep. I wish for the pain pills that were on my bedroom dresser. I didn't have Tracy to stop me this time and although I knew that it was something that I would have regretted later, I could think of nothing past the moment. I wished I could end it all.

Turning Point

I AWAKENED TO the distant sound of my cell phone going off in my purse. It was four thirty in the morning and Tracy was frantic. I lied and told her that I had stopped at Brian's and fell asleep.

My heart had wanted so much to tell her that I had been raped, but I wasn't ready. I was ashamed and knew that I was the one to blame for my downfall. The average person would've said that I asked for it. I even think I believed that I did.

"Brian called looking for you, Jae." She knew I was lying.

I didn't need to see the look on her face; I could hear it in her voice. She was my best friend; I was closer to her than the sisters I had, yet I wasn't able to confide in her.

I sighed in an attempt to speak.

"I...I'm sorry."

"What's going on Jae? And don't lie, I can tell that something has been different, but I left it up to you to tell me. You know you can tell me anything. At least, I thought you knew."

Tears filled my eyes as I wished that she was there to console me and give me the hug that I needed.

I not only let myself down, but I let her, my kids and Brian down and there was nothing that anyone could say or do to take it away.

"I'll be home as soon as I can." I told her as I hung up the phone.

Before returning home, I tried to call Mike to let him know what had happened. I wanted that son of a bitch to die for what he had done to me and I knew that once I told Mike, he was going to take of everything, whether he was a friend of his or not.

Despite the times that he said I disobeyed him, he was my pimp and he said that he would protect me from anyone who stepped out of line or messed with his money.

After my third call, I decided to give up assuming that he was busy taking care of some other business that needed his attention as well. Since it was obvious that my urgency was not important enough for him to return my call, I called no more and attempted to get the images of my horrible ordeal out of my head.

As I gathered my belongings to go home, my cell rings back. It was him and he was mad as hell.

"What do you want, Jae?" he asked with an attitude.

I began crying and telling him the story of how Derrick repeatedly raped me. He starts to laugh and then tells me to hold on. Unaware of what he was doing, I hold until a strange but familiar voice gets on the phone.

"Didn't I tell you that it was consensual?" he asked.

My hurt turned into anger as I tried to overcome the shock that he knew what had happened.

Hanging up the phone, I left the room in a rage while ignoring the pain that I was experiencing in an attempt to get home to where I felt at peace.

As I entered the house, I was surprised to find Tracy and the kids asleep in the living room. It was apparent that they were waiting on me, afraid that something terrible had happened.

I wanted to wake her to share with her my emotions, but I decided against it while I rushed to remove my filth.

I couldn't get the water hot enough although it scalded me terribly while leaving me helpless on my hands and knees. I sat on the floor allowing the water to beat on me while I cried until I could cry no more. After 30 minutes of shower torture, I finally stepped out once the water turned cold. I painfully struggled while applying my gown and crawled to the side of the bed as if I had been beaten before being sent to bed.

While on my knees I prayed that God would forgive me for the things that I had done. I had become a sinner and I needed forgiveness. I begged for him to lead me to the path of righteousness while showing me the way out of hell. It was apparent that I had strayed from the path that he had set for me and my eyes were now open to finally know the difference.

"Please help me to help myself and my kids. I love you Heavenly Father. Amen." I then crawled into bed.

Time For a Change

As I awakened, realizing that I was safely at home in my own bed, I tried to jump up to check on the kids to make sure they were okay. My pounding headache reminded me of my night of misery, and the thought of trying to tackle the day made me sick to the stomach.

I felt drunk, and as I attempted to get up out of bed, I noticed the bottle of pills that were lying beside me. Unable to stand to my feet, I called out for Tracy, ready to expose the truth.

Instead of awakening me, she left a note with Sasha stating that she would call later to check on me since it was obvious that I had a rough night. Preparing myself for her call, I prayed that I'd have the strength to tell her how rough life had been for me without feeling the shame that I was currently feeling.

"Momma, are you okay?" Sasha asked as she hovered over me.

It seemed as though she was a giant girl with a small voice. I rolled over placing the pillow over my head and mumbled from underneath.

"Give me just a minute. I don't feel too well."

I knew she suspected something was wrong, but I couldn't let her know just how wrong that something really was. While telling myself that it was not right for her to see me in the pathetic state that I was in, I sucked up every feeling that I had in me and attempted to get myself together.

I took them to school and the babysitter without breaking down as I relived the rape. I prayed over and over for constant direction although I knew that God had given me a wakeup call to get my life straight.

I knew what I needed to do not only for my sake, but for the kids as well, but for some reason, the money I made kept replaying in my head.

I began making excuses about what happened, assuming that it had to be something I did to make him treat me the way that he did. A small voice in the back of my mind reminded me that I would never again make the money that I was making now if I called it quits. I also thought about the things I was able to do for my family and a proud feeling overcame me, knowing that I was able to provide.

I tried to convince myself that since this was the first time that someone had ever taken advantage of me, there was a good chance that it would never happen again. Besides, I survived this long, so I felt there was no need to continue to sulk and complain.

Mike had finally come to his senses and apologized for not being there like he should've been. He told me that next time, I needed to just do as I was told so I wouldn't suffer as much.

"Remember, baby girl: you're paid to make us happy. Get over it, cause you know he wants you again." He said as he began removing my clothes.

He called himself repaying me for what I went through by trying to show me love.

It seemed as though each time we were together now, I hated myself even more than the first time we had sex. What was different this time was that while he took what he wanted, I didn't give in to what he wanted. I lay there doing nothing, as I wished that it was over – and this time, he made me feel worse than Derrick did.

The nights of my night life seemed longer than before, and the men that he had chosen for me seemed to get worse.

It was competitive on the streets and I finally realized that I had not been trained to handle the realities of the prostitution game. Some whores had their clicks; they'd make sure the ones that they were down for made their money's worth for the night. But since I was Mike's so-called "good bitch turned bad," they despised and looked down on me.

When I saw something that I liked or knew when someone was coming my way, they would jump in front of me and looked back like they dared me to speak up.

Knowing that I needed to make my money just as much as they

did theirs, I didn't raise a fuss. I wouldn't give them the satisfaction of thinking they were on top.

After watching how they worked, I taught myself how to get in with whomever I could. I became desperate and was willing to fuck anyone who was willing to fuck me, even it was only for a few measly dollars in a cheap ass motel.

I now understood why he told me that I should be grateful for him choosing the men I slept with, because the ones that I now had to deal with were just as nasty as I had seen myself to be. When the word got out that Mike wasn't as down for me as he once was, they considered me fair game, and took what they wanted.

"Girl, be careful with who you get in with. I know you need the money, but you have kids. Be there for *them*; they need you more than the money."

This female voice whispering in behind my ear belonged to someone I knew. I didn't yet dare turn around, though.

"Thanks, but why do you care? How do you know that I have kids? Who told you about me?" I questioned hoping that she would give me what I wanted, which was clue to who her identity was.

Instead of further elaborating, she walked away, allowing me to only see the back of her as she disappeared in the distance.

She had a small frame and was taller than me. Her hair was short and black, but many of us wore wigs as disguises. I figured she was wearing one as well. I wanted to run after her, but knew that since I was on unfamiliar territory, I probably shouldn't.

As I stood waiting for my next customer, my mind replayed her words. She was right; my kids did need me more than the money, but at the same time, I knew that without money, I had no life.

The night air was cold and the tiny skirt that I had on felt paper thin and served my butt and hips no purpose. My legs trembled as I walked briskly down the sidewalk in my newly purchased stilettos when a 2007 silver Jaguar pulled up in an attempt to rescue me from walking pneumonia.

"Thank God!" I mumbled while walking over to see who was going to make me the highest paid whore of the evening.

I straightened out the piece of clothing that I had on and swept my fingers through the wig that sat on top of my head.

As I stooped over to peer inside the darkened tinted windows that I hoped would eventually roll down, the back door on the passenger's side popped open.

As the door opened wider, I stepped back and allowed the owner of a well-toned female's leg step out of the car.

In an instant, I recognized that it was the same woman who cautioned me early on, and I was no longer as cold as I had been since my blood began racing through my veins. Instead of being afraid as to who she was, I became excited. She that was concerned for my safety, she that came back to make sure I was alright. She happened to be my friend from high school, Angela.

I jumped back once I noticed that it was her. My mouth dropped and I cupped my hand over it. I gasped in excitement as I started to give her a hug.

"Angela! Girl, what are you doing out here? How did you know I was here?" I questioned.

She looked at me with even wider eyes. "Me? No the question, is what are *you* doing here? C'mon Jae, why are you doing this?"

"You're better than this. Don't tell me that this is the reason that you called?" She asked in amazement.

I didn't know what to say.

"Come on, get in. We need to talk."

I was hesitant although I felt I needed to hear what she had to say. It was obvious she had been down the path that I was on, but in fear that the word would get out to Mike, I backed away.

"Look, I'll give you what you need for the night, just get in. It's crucial for you to hear me out."

It seemed as though we rode around for hours, but in reality it had only been an hour. She knew everything there was to know about Mike and the control that we allowed him to have over us. She told me that he was more dangerous than I could've ever imagined and that in order for me to get out, I would either have to kill him or move away.

"Girl, it's not safe, trust me. I wouldn't tell you wrong. The only reason I was fortunate enough to get away was because I knew someone crazier and more powerful than him on these streets."

I heard what she was saying and trusted her judgment, but it seemed as if something was missing, and I needed to know.

"So you were once his, too?"

"Yes Jae; I actually got caught up with him while still in high school. That's how I knew how to keep the men I was with. I knew how to please from experience."

She stopped as the car stopped.

"Here, take this. Get away from him and save your life as well as your soul."

As I got out, I told her thank you while taking the five hundred she offered. She told me that Mike would know that I didn't earn it if she gave me more than what she did. She said that since he knew the area that I had been in, he just about knew what I should've made. Mr. Brown was the name that she gave me to use in case he asked.

"When he asks, because I know he will, tell him that he has a mole on his right cheek." She winked and drove off.

In case someone happened to see me with her, I continued as his whore until I thought the time was right for me to get out.

I greatly appreciated her words of wisdom since she had been where I was. She made me feel even better about myself when I found out that in high school, she allowed me to hang with her since she often wished she could be like me. She admired my determination, but then apologized for allowing me to pick up her ways, which she believed got me in trouble. She told me that this was her way of giving me back what she felt she took from me.

As time went on, I was hit, choked and raped more times than I could count. I hid my bruises well from Tracy and the kids and the times that I had to work over to make the money Mike demanded, I found myself lying, saying that I had to work over barely making it at home in time enough for Tracy to go where she needed to go.

I was mentally drained and realized that I was no longer able to give the love to my kids that I had when I was broke. I found Tracy questioning my distance, saying that she knew there was something going on and often tried to demand the truth out of me. Knowing that she was on my side and that she would love me regardless of who I had become, I continued to lie and tell her that I was okay and she just had to trust my word.

I became fed up and came to the decision that I could no longer degrade myself the way that I had been. Regardless of how well off I had become and how much of a better life I had made for my kids, I knew that they would not like seeing the mother they looked up to degrading herself while selling her soul to have more.

Despite the fear of not knowing what Mike was going to do to me, I made up my mind that I was going to tell Brian and Tracy the truth.

I was ready for whatever Brian wanted to do with our relationship, and ready for the disappointment that Tracy was going to have towards me. I was tired of living a lie, tired of being disrespected, and most of all, tired of failing my kids.

Fearless

BEFORE MIKE caught wind of what I was going to do, I knew I had to tell Brian the truth before Mike did. Prepared to open up to him, I headed his way as if I was in a hurry but was later side tracked by a phone call from my mother.

I had recently made my way back into their lives since they saw I was doing well for myself. I had repaid them and other members of my family the debt I owed to them and we began reconciling the problems that I caused.

I even phoned my sister once I decided to give up the night life.

She thought I was again calling for money to help out with the rent as before, but instead I surprised her with something completely different.

Since she was the lawyer in the family, I asked her to draw up my will. She asked why I was asking, but again, I couldn't tell her. I asked her to trust my judgment while keeping it in her possession until the family needed it. Knowing that I was still the same bull headed sister that I had been for many years, she left well enough alone and told me that she loved me.

I knew that she couldn't keep her mouth closed and as soon as I asked, the quicker our mother found out. She had kept it a secret that she knew what I asked for until now.

"Jaelynn Marie Stone, how dare you! Is this the reason why you asked your sister to draw you up a will?" She scolded as she asked a question.

She had not exactly told me why she was as furious as she was; therefore I said nothing until I knew for sure that she knew.

"Ma, calm down. What are you fussing about?"

"Your father is in jail over you and your crazy ways. That's where all this money has been coming from ain't it?" She hollered.

I knew that she indeed knew and tried to ask how they found out. She was beside herself and stuttered with every other word. She was hurt and despite how proud she had once been over my comeback, she quickly became resentful.

"I will go to bail him out. Everything will be okay, you have to trust me." I said before hanging up.

I wanted to get downtown before anyone else did. Besides, I wanted to hear from him exactly how he found out, and wanted to be sure that Brian still didn't know.

My father told me that while he was playing chess with some neighbors of his, a stepson of his neighbors came by making a fuss about what he had heard. I happened to be the topic of conversation brought up by one of my customers who was a friend of a friend to his stepson.

Furious, my father retrieved a gun from his car and pulled it on everyone who found it even slightly amusing. Although no one was hurt, the police were called and off he went.

After constant searching and phone calls, Brian was nowhere to be found for days after he heard about the dispute between my family and me. I assumed that he knew since it was unlike him to not even return calls left by the kids, but I couldn't blame him for the hurt that I knew he felt.

My soul was empty and my heart ached continuously. My life had made a drastic change and it felt as though it was spiraling down the drain. I ended up confiding in Tracy believing that she deserved to know the truth. She cried as I vividly shared the hurt and pain that comes with tricking. She held me in her arms until her arms were tired, stating that she suspected that something was wrong, and assumed that if it was really bad, I would've told her instead of fighting the battle by myself.

"Jae, I am so sorry for what you've had to go through." She said sympathetically. "So, how are we going to fix this?"

I had no idea. Trying to make a joke out of the situation I replied, "Run away?"

I smirked while resting my head on her shoulder waiting for her next response.

"Seriously, from what I hear, it doesn't seem as though Mike is anyone to mess with, and...you know as well as I do, you may end up losing Brian."

She was right, my chances for keeping Brian in my life was slim to none. I had rehearsed my lines over and over as to what I was going to say to him. In my heart I knew that no matter how many times I tried to make it sound good, nothing was going to be good enough to keep him. I hated to lose the only man I ever loved, but if I had no choice, then that's how it was and I deserved to be alone.

Ready, but afraid of what lied ahead, I went to tell Brian about my deception. Although we had become distant, and I was unaware of what plans he may have made for the night, I went to find him before it was too late.

I left a message for Mike as well letting him know that I was no longer afraid of him and that if he threatened or tried to do harm to me or my kids that I would go to the police and sing like a canary.

Truthfully, I was scared to death, and I knew that if I ran into Mike, it was definitely going to be the death of me.

"Look Brian, answer the phone, I know you're there. I need to talk you tonight, it's very important. Please call me back," I begged.

It was the sixth message I left for him. I tried calling his cell phone, but his voicemail automatically came on. As I started getting nervous, wondering if Mike had gotten to him before I did, Tracy encouraged me to go to his place to see if he was home.

"I'll go with you if you need me to," she said, supportively.

Not wanting to put her in harm's way, I opted to go by myself and asked her to call the police if she hadn't heard anything from me within an hour.

"Tell the kids I love them and I'll be home shortly." I said, leaving the house.

"Be careful," she cautioned as I headed to beg my man for the forgiveness I didn't deserve.

A Love to Die For

As I pulled into the complex, thoughts of finding Brian engaged in some type of activity with another woman raced through my mind. My heart raced as I grew closer to the door and I felt the anxiety I had experienced when I had left the hospital.

"Calm down, Jae," I kept telling myself. "Everything will be okay."

Once I stepped within inches from his door, I noticed something different. I heard a voice, a familiar one, which quickly put fear in my heart.

My body was telling me to turn and walk away, but my mind was telling me to face my fear and do what I had intended to do.

As I raised my fist to knock at the door, the door opened as if they were expecting me. Mike was the one I saw first and greeted me with sarcasm.

"Well who do we have here, Ms. Jae. You are so predictable."

The door was opened wide enough for me to see that Brian was not in sight. Music was playing in the background, and the aroma of tacos mixed with cologne filled the air. My first thought was to run and forget about what I had came for, but as I attempted to back away from the door, he grabbed my arm and pulled me closer into him.

"Why run now? It's evident you came for something," he insisted.

I decided not to struggle since I knew it would worsen the situation. Instead, I stayed where he had me, hoping that Brian would come to save me.

As Brian entered the living room, I could tell that he was amazed to find Mike sitting beside me fondling my breast while I just sat as though it was okay.

"Hey man, what the hell's going on? And why are you just sitting there allowing him to touch you like that?" he asked, coming over to where we were sitting.

I wanted so much to jump up and ask him to remove me from harm's way, but knowing what was in my best interest, I stayed and attempted to speak in my defense.

"Brian, baby listen to me, it's not what you think. He... he..." I stuttered afraid of going further.

Mike turned towards me and questions, "He what, Jae?"

Brian held his hand out for me to take hold. With relief, I sighed while looking at Mike for approval. I had no idea as to what I was going to do if he told me I had to stay, but regardless, I knew I had to obey.

With a nod of his head, I grabbed Brian's hand and pulled him back into the bedroom while pleading for him to listen to me. His body felt warm as I rubbed against him. He had just stepped out of the shower and I could smell the mixture of the soap and his cologne. I didn't want to mess up his nicely pressed clothes, but I had other things in mind and keeping him together was far from it.

"What's wrong with you? Why are you here?" he asked, with a look in his eyes like he didn't know me.

I sat on the bed, hoping that he would follow my lead.

"I have something to tell you. Please understand where I am coming from before you start making judgments."

I dropped to my knees as I held his hand in hopes that I could get out what I wanted to say before Mike cut me off.

"Baby, I..."

Tears rolled down my eyes before I could even begin. The look in his eyes told me that he was just as afraid to hear what I needed to say as I was to tell him.

"Forgive me for the pain that I have caused you, the humiliation that you will soon know about. I did it for us, for my kids."

I stopped and slumped over in a stupor. I couldn't go on although I knew I now had to.

He sat on the bed and picked me up while wrapping his arms around me.

"Whatever it is Jae, it's okay. Just tell me, I'm here for you....forever." He said trying to comfort me.

With that, I felt I had enough confirmation: he was not going to leave, regardless of what I was about to tell. Our love was stronger than I could ever imagine and for this, I had to be strong.

As we held each other, I caught a glimpse of the shower that seemed to peer at me in the eyes. It reminded me of the many times we had shared one another while promising that we would never let anything or anyone come between us.

As I dazed off, recalling past memories, he begged for my attention.

"Hello, earth to Jae. Are you still here?" he joked as he waved his hand in my face.

While opening my mouth to answer, the bedroom door flew open.

"Now, I know you are not about to tell our little secret are you?" Mike asked, almost squealing.

Walking to the bed, he stands in front of Brian as if he were going to confront him and then speaks again.

"You ready to hear her secret?"

Brian stands to face his demon and then looks at me before looking back at Mike.

"What secret? Man you betta go on with that bullshit. Jae doesn't keep secrets, and she doesn't lie."

Mike laughs and then turns to me to ask if that's true.

I stand, peering in Brian's eyes, hoping that his concentration was kept on me. With sweaty palms, I take his hands in mine and began telling him the untold lies that I had hidden from him.

Shaking his head as if he didn't want to hear anymore, he pushed me away with each attempt that I made to get closer.

"Brian you have to believe me. I did this for us, for my kids. My life was hell before I met you. But when you came along, it seemed as though my prayers had been answered."

He walked away as if he didn't care of what else I had to say while talking in the distance.

"What does that have to do with becoming a whore? You were supposed to be mine and only mine, Jae. What the hell did you do?!" he hollered, as his eyes rimmed with tears.

"I didn't want you to take care of us. I wanted to somehow take care of you. I wanted to repay you for being the man that we needed," I cried.

Fed up with our exchange, Mike interrupted with clapping. He was applauding my speech.

"And you finally get the nerve to tell Brian that you were the whore that I so often claimed you to be. See Brian, I told you in the beginning that she was a good catch." He laughs.

He continued by telling Brian that he was not the only one who had been fortunate to get a piece of me. While naming all the customers that he claimed he sold me to, he went on to mention how much money he made in return for the ass that he now called his. He pierced into Brian's heart the best way he knew how and looked at him fiercely as he dared him to do anything in return.

Not afraid of what was being dished out to him, Brian grew angry and shot back the remarks that were brewing in his head.

"You were supposed to be my boy. I never once thought you'd be jealous of what I had. I gotta give it to you though. You took trash out of my own garbage can."

Without backing down, Mike stepped to his defense and faced him as if they were about to kiss.

"Whoa now, big boy, it ain't my fault I was smart enough to know a good piece of meat when I smelled it. It was like taking candy from a baby, no pun intended," he growled.

Trying to take the conversation in another direction, I stepped in between them to break up the hostility.

I tell Brian that Mike wasn't worth it, and that I could handle him on my own.

"Yeah go on and handle him like you've been doing. I have no further use for you," he scowls, pulling away from me.

I forget that Mike was there and pour my heart out as a last resort.

"Brian! Listen to me, I love you remember, I just had to do what I needed to survive!"

He looked me dead in the eye and without blinking told me, "Whatever I had was yours. Regardless of how much you and the kids needed, I had your back. You were just too proud to accept it. So now, it's on you."

I could see the tears in his eyes, but refusing to let me see more, he turned away and headed out of the bedroom leaving Mike and me alone.

Forgetting that he left his phone in the bathroom, Brian reenters the room, making note of how close Mike and I were standing.

I again tried to plead with him before Mike grabbed my wrist.

"Leave him alone, Jae. Didn't you hear him say he had no more use for you?"

Brian briskly walks over to Mike and punches him in the jaw. Before anything else could take place, Mike pulls a gun from inside of his jeans and aims it at Brian's head.

Brian becomes motionless and silent as he now knows his place. Remaining calm, he looks at me as if he knows that the end for him is coming. While biting his bottom lip, a tear falls from his eye before he whispers the words "I Love You."

In an attempt to plead with Mike, I beg for him to leave, telling him that I'd even leave with him if he wanted me to.

He then takes his opposite hand and backslaps me across my face. I fall into the nightstand, hitting my head on the edge, causing a gash in my forehead.

As blood gushed down my face and onto the floor, I attempted to get up before realizing that without help, it was useless.

"Brian, please help me," I whined.

As much as I thought I wanted his help, I knew that leaving was in his best interest—and I wanted him to leave. I had a feeling that things were going to turn bad, and I didn't want him getting caught up in the drama that I had caused.

With the gun still pointed to his head, he walked towards me holding out his hand for me to take hold. Instead of allowing me to reach for his, Mike offered his instead.

"He has no use for you remember?" he reminds me again.

While taking hold of Mike's hand as I knew best, I began thinking about the life that I had grown to demise.

I thought about the accomplishments that I had made in my life, although small, and how happy I made my kids just by loving and spending time with them. I thought about the sacrifices that I made for them just to see them smile and how happy they were when I could only give them love.

"Please Mike..." I begged.

"Whatever it is that you want, I'll give," I seductively whispered.

I kneeled down beside him and put my hands together as if I was praying. As my voice became weary and I began to stutter, I tried to make peace with him.

"You are better than this. Who am I to come between that?" I questioned as I kept my eyes on him.

Brian stood motionless as if his feet were glued to the floor and as I prayed that he wouldn't interrupt, I continued on.

"I have kids at home…they need me, and they need him. Please just let us go." I begged.

He listened and then spoke as if he felt pity.

"Yeah, you're right, Jae. We were one of a kind before you came along. But, now that you're here, that's all changed. Let me show you how." He said as if he were trying to prove a point.

I looked at him with resentment not knowing what he had in mind. He turned the gun on me and pulled me up from my knees.

As I stood in front of him, he began ripping my shirt off my chest with his left hand. Exposing my bare breast, he took one in the palm of his hand and began playing with my nipples.

With nipples erected from the chill that had crossed their way, he started sucking them as if he were an infant being nursed. I became angry at myself for allowing him to treat me this way, and at Brian for not standing up to him despite the gun he once had pointed on him.

The tension in the room could be felt as Brian looked on helplessly. Blood continued to stream down my face as I tasted the bitterness of each drop that fell into my mouth. As I reached to wipe my lips, Mike pulled me by my hair in fear that I was trying to do something stupid.

"Hey Mike, chill!" Brian yelled out.

While looking at him as if he were waiting for Brian to get the nerve to charge, he threw me on the bed to prepare to get what he wanted.

He told Brian that if he was smart, he'd let him be and let him finish getting a piece of me.

"Naw, man, can't let you do that," Brian said as he stood even straighter.

"Excuse you? What? You choose her over me…your boy?" Mike questioned.

Without hesitation, Brian answered fearlessly.

"Yes sir. Not letting it go down like that. I love her too much to stand and let you disrespect her like that. Do what you gotta do to me, but not her."

I couldn't believe the words that were coming from his mouth. Despite everything that he had just learned about me, he was still willing to defend me.

"Just like a bitch. Yo ass must be whipped."

"Bitch or not, nigga, you're going to leave her alone. Be a real man about your shit. This is why I got you beat in the game. I know how to handle business the right way. I can do it without beating my bitches the way you do." Brian said.

So this was it! It wasn't about me. Mike didn't lure me into the game for his pleasure; it was all about the competition. Mike was jealous for not being the man that Brian was.

As Brian casually walked over to give me a blanket, a single shot was fired.

Brian fell backwards onto the floor with eyes open trying to mumble the words "get out." Being unable to hear him, I struggled to read his lips.

I ran to his side trying to keep him from closing his eyes. Inspecting his body as if I were a nurse, I tried to see where he had been shot. With his eyes, he was telling me that Mike was near.

I looked up to see Mike's large body towering over us with his gun again pointed at Brian. It wasn't over. He wanted Brian to know that he was in control and with his second shot, if Brian didn't know it, I now did.

I jumped up as if I were the one in control and began hitting at him asking how he could be so selfish.

I cried uncontrollably while going back to Brian's side and holding my hands over the left side of his chest. I was determined to apply as much pressure as I needed to keep him from bleeding to death. Keeping him alive was the only thought in my mind and regardless of what Mike had planned for me, I was going to make sure that I stayed by Brian's side until he took his last breath.

His breathing became shallow and his eyes were becoming heavy.

"Hang on baby, help is on the way." I said as I scrambled for the phone.

"You can't leave me. I need you, I…I… promise I'll do better and will be the woman you want me to be."

It was hopeless. The moment I promised that I would be who he wanted me to be, I watched him take his last breath and I knew he was gone.

Breathless

WHILE LYING beside him, Mike bent over to pick me up by grasping the hair on the crown of my head.

"What kind of woman will you be for me now that he's gone?" he asked.

Without even thinking I spit in his face and attempted to fight for my life.

"I hate you, I hate you, I hate you! I will never be anything to you or for you. You are nothing to me. You will never be what Brian was to me!" I exclaimed.

He again threw me down except this time on the floor next to Brian's helpless body. Placing the gun to the side of us, he ripped my pants off as if he was a dog in heat. In hopes that someone who had to hear the gunshots ring out would come, I lay there while he took total control of my body like the mad man that he was.

His grunts were as frightening as his actions and as he took the last part of my soul, I turned my head to Brian wishing that I was in the same place as he was.

When finished, he got up and ordered me to do the same. He told me I needed to clean myself up before the police arrived. He said that he had to leave and take care of some business, but I needed to wait to tell them that I was trying to defend myself. As I started walking to the bathroom he stopped me in my tracks and placed the gun in my hand so that my fingerprints could be placed on the gun.

"If you try to do anything stupid, you'll be next," he said.

Doing exactly what he said, I rubbed my hands over the gun and pulled the trigger. As much as I hated being the one who took the life of another, I felt this was something that I needed to do. Indeed it was self defense.

As he stumbled backwards, I dropped the gun not knowing what to do next. I scrambled to get dressed while heading to the living room to grab my purse. Then, as I headed toward the door, I felt the gun on back of my head.

"Damnit, the bastard wasn't dead," I thought, and before I could turn around, he fired one shot to the back of my head.

I collapsed. My head was pounding and I had the worst headache ever. As blood now poured from my head, I placed my hand to the back of my head to see how much damage was done.

Refusing to give up while being faced with death, it was then that I realized I had something to live for. I told myself that since death was imminent, it was time for me to die while trying to live.

Attempting to pick myself up from the floor, I brought my arms to the side of me and began lifting myself up from the floor. As I rose, the second shot was fired at the base of my neck, blood poured out and from the immediate blood loss, I went limp and knew that I was soon headed where my Brian was.

Silence filled the room and I concentrated on the erratic beating of my heart. It felt as though it was trying to escape from my body, and I knew I was going to die. As I listened for more, it became evident that I was near death when I heard how shallow my breathing was starting to become. And, when I collapsed, my lungs did as well.

"Bitch, wake up!" he yelled, as he would often say after a long night on the streets.

As I felt the slap of his hand on the side of my face, I also felt a pull of my arm. He was attempting to drag me to the couch in hopes that I would get up.

He was mentally sick and I knew that if I didn't attempt to do as he said, he would for sure finish me off.

"Get up, bitch!" he angrily demanded.

Despite what he wanted, or how much he yelled and pulled on me, there was nothing I could do. I couldn't obey even if I wanted to, so there I lay motionless and drained knowing that my last breath was soon to follow.

I struggled between each breath that I took with tears escaping each eye. I knew that my time had come despite how hard I fought.

I begged God to let me hang on a few minutes more until helped arrived. I began bargaining and telling him that if he allowed me to live, I would get my life in order to become a testimony for others.

As I tried to stay awake, I recited a scripture that came to mind. Psalms 46:10: "Be still and know that I am God." I continued to repeat that verse until it seemed as if God had taken over and began whispering it in my ear for me. I then knew that the only way that I was going to survive was by the grace of God, so I obeyed him and stayed still.

Wake Up Call

I FELT A soft and gentle hand feel the side of my neck. She was feeling for my pulse.

"She's alive, but I don't know for how long. We need to intubate," a female voice says.

"Her pulse is thready; we're going to lose her if we don't move quickly," she said in a soft but confident tone that allowed me to relax. I knew I was in good hands.

As I rode in the ambulance to the hospital, the fluids flowing through my I.V. felt as though they were bringing life back into me. I felt the warmth of the fluids traveling up my veins. I believed I had a second chance, but then realized that my time was running out.

"We need to intubate, you think you can do it?" she asked.

As they attempted to provide an airway for me, I knew they were struggling.

"Too much blood. I can't see. Dammit, it's not going in."

"Put a move on it Josh, we need to get her there before we lose her."

As the ride continued, their words became nonsensical and their sentences started fading in and out. While rushing me into the hospital, I could hear them telling the E.R. doctor that my blood pressure was dropping.

"Give her another 2 liter bolus of normal saline," a husky voice replied.

"Were losing her, prepare to get the defibrillator…"

As they shocked life back into me, I started seeing my life from the birth of my children until present. What was God telling me? Was he allowing me to see the blessings he had placed in my life and only for me to realize how quickly they disappear with greed? Or was he preparing me for the life to come? A life-changing moment was taking place, and from this point on, I knew that if I turned my life over to God, he would give me the desires of my heart.

"Twenty-five year old African-American female. Gunshot wound to the head by unknown suspect. B/P 60/40 palpable," a female voice calmly reported. I heard scrambling and movement all around me. They were moving quickly as if they didn't have much time to save my life. I couldn't see anything, and the words that were audible started to become distant. The voices were slowly fading away.

"B/P is dropping. We're losing her—she's coding! Everyone clear."

I heard a familiar voice orchestrating the efforts to save my life. They worked feverishly to save me, and once I heard the attending say "Job well done," I knew that I could continue fighting.

"Is she perfusing well?" I heard someone ask.

"Yes doctor. Cap refill less than 3. Skin pink, warm and dry."

They stabilized me long enough to allow the O.R. to prepare for surgery. As I was transported to the SICU, I heard the nurse give the report to another nurse on the unit.

"Gunshot wound to head with intrachymal hemorrhaging. She had a craniotomy with one drain placement. Vital signs currently stable, Mannitol infusing as ordered with a Propofol drip as well…"

As they settled me in the room, I heard one of the nurses talking with someone in the background.

"She's stable, but we can only allow one visitor at this time. Be sure they are aware that they can't stay the night," she said.

I heard the nurse position herself at the side of my bed and then attempted to quietly sit at the foot. I assumed that she was documenting my progress and vitals since she had to monitor me closely.

Knowing that I was in good hands along with the Lords, I relaxed my mind and gave thanks to him for bringing me thus far.

Shortly after arriving in the room, I heard Tracy's voice.

"Can she hear me?" She asked the nurse.

The nurse answered, "Yes."

"What is that in her mouth?"

"Ms. Stone is intubated. It is a tube that basically does the breathing for her. She is sedated as well, so she won't over-breathe the machine."

Tracy thanked her and then asked, "Could I please um….be alone with her for a few minutes?"

As she left the room, Tracy came beside me and whispered in my ear.

"I am so sorry for letting you go. I am even sorrier for what has happened to you. I know in my heart that you will get through this. I love you, Sis," she cried.

I heard her sniffle as she gently started stroking my face and hair. She continuously apologized for the incident placing responsibility on her for not calling the police as soon as she had promised had I not been home or called her like I asked her to.

If only I could tell her that it was okay.

She was a God send to me and the kids when there was no one else. Unfortunately, I hadn't thanked her enough for being our support when I had been down.

As she stood by my side, the nurse re-entered the room and stood by hers.

"Are you okay ma'am?" She calmly asked attempting to comfort her.

"No! I'm not…because she's not…is she? I mean, she's bad, isn't she?" Tracy sniffles again before blowing her nose.

"What's her prognosis? Did you know that she has children who need her and a faithful man that loves…" she stops.

I could hear her scrambling in her purse as if she was in search of something that she obviously couldn't find.

Confused about what she was doing, the nurse asks, "What's wrong? Did you misplace something? Can I help you find something?"

Tracy turns around and answers, "Yes…I mean no. Never mind that. Look—did they tell you what actually happened at the crime scene? Was hers the only body that was found?"

Not really knowing what else to say, the nurse responds.

"I'm sorry—that's not our concern. Anyway, if I did know, I couldn't disclose that information to you because of the privacy laws. Maybe you can talk to…"

Before she was able to finish her sentence, an alarm started sounding. Without hesitation, the nurse moves Tracy out of the way to get a closer look at the machine that was somewhere near the head of my bed.

"What's going on? What's wrong with her? Is she okay?" Tracy questioned in a panic.

"Yes, she's alright, the alarm sounds when her vitals are below or above the settings that we have set for her. Her blood pressure went up, but it's coming down. I'm sorry, but you'll have to leave now. Maybe you can come back tomorrow?"

Before leaving, Tracy again came to my side and placed her hands on mine. She promised to take care of the kids until I came home and told me that they were okay and at her mother's house.

"I'll send your love to them, until you're able to do so yourself. I'll be back tomorrow. I love you much." She finished before kissing my cheek.

As she was leaving out the door, she was greeted by a soft but confident spoken lady that had sounded to be in her mid fifties. She introduced herself as the chaplain and wanted to see if Tracy needed some spiritual guidance at this time.

Unsure of whether she accepted the offer since their voices headed off into the distance, I prayed for Tracy and that she accepted her consolation since I knew that without faith in God, it would be even harder for Tracy to deal with this.

While praying, I directed all the energy I had into staying in tune with God. I had the faith of a mustard seed and believed that he would give me the desires of my heart as long as I continued to trust in Him and show gratitude for everything that He had given.

God had given me another chance to show him that I was grateful and that regardless of the situations that may have arisen, I would always know that He was in control.

The energy in the room became powerful as I spoke to Him and I felt His greatness. All things were working together for the good of God and for that, I was thankful.

"How's she doing?" Dr. David questioned.

While standing at my side, he became quiet.

"Neurosurgery performed the craniotomy and evacuated her hematoma. ICP is coming down. Her prognosis is fair," another voice stated.

"Paralysis?" Dr. David questioned.

"Looks that way, unfortunately. The bullet that hit the base of her neck, shattered her first and second vertebrae."

I could tell that Dr. David was still in the room. Unsure of what he was doing, I listened for more.

"Excuse me; are you the doctor taking care of her?" Tracy asked.

"I'm sorry, no I am not. I work in the E.D. Can I help you?"

"No. I'll return later," she says.

After a few minutes longer, he left the room but not before placing a gentle kiss on my forehead.

As he did in the apartment, I once again heard God speak to me, but this time in a bold and confident tone.

"I am here not only holding your hand, but your mind, body and soul."

I continued to listen as he gave me comfort.

As I took deep breaths in an effort to breath over the vent, I felt the warm air move into my lungs. With my mind focused on movement, my toes and fingertips began to tingle.

As each day had passed, I seemed to make better progress than the days before. The swelling surrounding my brain started decreasing, and they were discussing the option of replacing my skull.

I was apprehensive about surgery but knew that since I had been medically stable my chances for a better recovery were well on its way.

Unsure of what legal matters needed to be handled on my behalf, Tracy called my sister to ask for advice.

"She already has them in order. She called months ago asking me to take care of it. I guess she knew that this life would get her," my sister stated.

Tracy was already emotional, but when finding out that something bad could be the end result, she broke down.

"So you're sure everything else is in order? The consent forms, DPOA and all that stuff?" Tracy nervously questioned.

I could tell when she was nervous because whenever she was, every word her voice let out, squeaked.

"Yep, it's all good. I just wished I could've been here sooner. You shouldn't have had to deal with this on your own. I know you two are closer than we are, but Tracy...she's my sister," Jade stated.

There was silence in the room and as I waited for someone to speak, he entered the room.

"Hi, I'm Dr. David. You must be Ms. Stones' sister."

Her voice boasted professionalism, and with a touch of a Texan drawl. She responded,

"Yes, I'm Jade, nice to meet you. Are you her surgeon?"

He smiled before answering.

"No, but I know her well and just wanted to come by as a support."

Clearing his throat, he explained that he was confident that I was more than stable, but as with any surgery, there was always the chance for complications.

"I know they will take care of her as best as they can. I'll have someone keep you abreast of how she's doing in surgery."

Jade and Tracy kissed me while leaving their tears on my face.

Jade told me that although my mother and father wanted to see me before I headed to surgery; they had to pick up Monique from the airport. She promised they would be here when it was over and that they loved me as much as she did.

After surgery, I was transferred back to SICU for further monitoring until I was more stable. The care that I received was more than I had expected.

The nurses ensured that I was going to be a walking miracle. Every night before their shift ended, one would come and pray for me while giving me the encouragement that I needed.

After my tenth day in SICU, the doctors felt that I was stable enough to be transferred to a private room. It allowed my family to have the opportunity to stay as long as they wanted, which allowed me to have the love and support that I needed to heal.

Monique and Jade stayed in town for a week before heading back home. Although they both admitted to having tight schedules, they both promised to fly down whenever needed if anything changed.

Jade was my power of attorney and was to be informed of any changes. I felt safe knowing that Dr. Wilson, my primary physician, had informed his staff of her expertise in legal matters. From that point on, I knew my care was going to be carefully monitored.

As my sisters left, my heart ached for them just as it did when they left for college. I thought about how long it would've been for me to have seen them again if I hadn't been shot. I made a promise to myself that once I left out of the hospital, it would never be that long again.

"Jae, can you hear me?" Dr. Wilson asked, while shining a small light in my eye. I gently moved my head as if I was trying to move away from the light.

"That-a-girl. Follow the light," he insisted.

The kids rushed to the side of the bed, screaming, "Momma's coming back! She's gonna be okay, ain't she?" Sasha screamed.

Dr. Wilson cautioned everyone to not get so excited, but stated that he felt optimistic about my recovery. He said that they would continue to monitor me and inform my family of any changes that came about.

Before leaving the room, he took my hand in his and told me to continue being strong since there were many people waiting for my recovery. As I attempted to give a smile, I gently squeezed his hand right back.

Keeping the Faith

SOME NIGHTS were worse than others during my recovery. I had been hospitalized for three months and although it was evident that I was recovering, I still had days that seemed to take me twenty steps backwards.

My blood pressure had risen on several occasions and to keep it controlled, they often gave me medications that were supposed to help. Dr. Wilson had ordered several tests to rule out cardiac problems including lab work called cardiac enzymes that they had to obtain every 6 hours when I had the misfortunate chest pains.

The medical team seemed to think it was due to the pain that I had probably been experiencing. Therefore they increased my PCA dosage and followed my pressure closely to see if it would change.

I wanted so much to tell them that I was not in as much pain as they assumed; I knew the elevation was due to the anxiety that I was experiencing as I mourned Brian.

The night of the incident constantly replayed in my head as I thought about how different things could have been if I would have just stayed home. I was to blame for Brian's death, and for so many other mistakes.

There were many nights that I suffered from dreams that brought me back to that night, on my knees, with Mike pointing the gun to my face threatening to shoot me at point blank range.

I even had dreams of Mike forcing me to repeatedly shoot Brian before turning the gun on myself.

Twenty eight days had passed after leaving the SICU and, although I was still hospitalized, my prognosis had improved. I was able to talk with my eyes by looking up to say yes and looking down to say no. I tired very easily, but knew that I was getting stronger every day.

Dr. David came to visit just as much as my family and when it was time for him to leave to start his shift in the emergency room, my anxiety often returned as I knew I was going to miss him as soon as he left.

The connection that I felt during our first meeting was as real as I assumed it to be.

He came by to visit at least three times a day, and when the kids were there with Tracy, he blended like he was family as if he was supposed to be there.

He talked to me about his life, and helped me try to figure out mine.

"I believe in you Jae, so believe in yourself and know that this too shall pass. I love you." He whispered in my ear as Brian used to do.

Tracy noticed the connection and instead of cautioning me as she first did, she told me she was happy for me. I always knew that she was in my corner, but her blessing meant the world. She wasn't just a friend; she was a true sister.

Dr. Wilson had informed me that after consulting with neurology, there wasn't too much hope that I would ever walk again, and for awhile, I believed that he knew best. As the days passed by, I continued to believe in miracles and tell myself that I one day was going to be able to walk out as a changed woman. Daily, while focused on movement, I constantly told myself that I was going to overcome the current state I was in.

I meditated and prayed every night and day, knowing in my heart that a miracle was going to happen. I practiced the law of attraction.

Believing that we are a magnetic force within the universe and that we attract the energy that we put out into the universe, I knew that I could have whatever it was that I wanted in life as long as I believed and was willing to receive.

There were many days that I often became discouraged, since I didn't see improvement. But I knew that if I thought negatively, negative things would happen. So, as bad as I may have felt, I quickly changed my negative thoughts to positive ones so I could attract healing and happiness.

When I when was discouraged, I knew that it stemmed from being dependent on others to take care of me. I was helpless and could do nothing for myself and to make matters worse, it was embarrassing to know that I needed someone to care of the private parts that, for months, belonged to everyone but me.

"Are you okay Jaelynn?" She asked as she prepared to clean me up.

I was silent and didn't want to offend her. I knew that Tasha, the nurses' assistant, would take good care of me as she often did before. But this day was different. I felt my dignity was gone and I again reminisced about my past life.

"Just thinking of my life and how it could have been different," I softly said.

"I understand, but look what you have now."

I looked at her in a confused state as if she was on another planet.

"What do I have Tasha? Look at me, tell me what do I have?" I asked with tears forming in my eyes.

She knew all about my past life, as I had often confided in her when she had bathed me before. As I cried, she would wipe away the tears that had begun to visit daily.

"You have your mind, your family that loves you and a testimony to encourage others by when you get out of here. Every day that I see you, you inspire me and I thank you for that. Oh, and not to mention that *fine ass* Dr. Allen David," she exclaimed.

Lifting my head up, I playfully ask her what she was talking about.

"Come on. Everybody sees it. You two are made for one another. The way you two look at one another when he visits, it's obvious you're in love! Besides, there is not a single doctor in this hospital who just comes to visits patients for the hell of it. He practically lives in this room when he's not on duty."

As I thought about what she had said, I leaned back with a smile knowing that she was exactly right. Despite the cards that I had been dealt, I was truly and gratefully blessed.

A Gift Returned

As my therapist came to work with me, I decided that I was going to focus my mind on movement with my toes since I had done it before while I was alone.

Hours earlier, I had been given a sponge bath and wanted to keep my socks off since I became easily hot. While assisting me with some passive range of motion, she noticed that I wiggled my toes without purposefully doing so.

"Oh my gosh, Ms. Stone, did you see that?!" she exclaimed.

She stood and ran to the door and flailed her arms for the other nurse to come in. Unsure about what was happening, three employees fled into the room.

"What's going on? Is she okay?" another nurse asked.

"Yes, she's alright. She moved her toes! Do it again, Jae, wiggle your toes!" she demanded.

After showing them that I was able to move my toes when asked, they notified Dr. Wilson and Dr. David and they came up within minutes. Standing back, Dr. Wilson stood back to watch as he instructed me to do it again.

"Ms. Stone, you are one determined young lady. How about we immediately move you to our rehab floor? The sooner the better," he insisted.

The next day, they started aggressive therapy with hopes that I would regain movement of my lower extremities. I shared a room with a woman slightly older than me who had been confined to a wheelchair since her motor vehicle accident.

Discouraged about therapy, since her pain had often gotten the best of her, she turned to me in despair, seeking guidance.

"I don't get it. How can you have so much faith?"

With tears in my eyes as well, I shared my thoughts.

"If you had been through what I've been through, you'd have every reason to be faithful. I've have truly been blessed, and from this point on, I know I have to keep looking for greater things."

As she prepared to question me again, Dr. David walks into the room. Noticing that he wasn't smiling, I knew that something was wrong.

"Hey you. What's going on? Why the look?" I questioned.

"Jae, the police are here. They need to ask you questions about the shootings," he said as he sat on the edge of my bed.

I was unprepared and unsure if I wanted to talk, but knew I had no choice and asked him to allow me some time with the officers.

They informed me that they had kept the investigation on hold in an attempt to allow me to recover, but now since I had improved; it was time to continue.

They were kind and sympathetic about what happened. They somehow knew that I had been framed by the way the fingerprints were on the gun.

"How could you tell?" I asked, relieved.

"The way they were scattered, it was clearly evident that it wasn't you. But of course there were other things that confirmed our investigation as well."

They said they also traced the registration of the gun back to a friend of Mike's and were confident that he was the culprit behind the whole, ugly scene.

They apologized for having to make me relive the incident, but needed to be able to close the file.

Before I allowed them to leave the room, I was determined to find out the answer to the question I'd been dying to ask.

"Officer?" I called out.

They both turned around eyeing me as if they were this time unprepared to answer my question.

"How many bodies were found? And whose were they?" I asked as I looked back and forth at them.

"Two ma'am. Unfortunately, we are unable to release the names. I'm sure that you can find out, though," the tallest one said as he smiled and followed the other one out.

With a sigh of relief, I thanked them for being polite and encouraged them to have a nice day.

Allen returned to the room to make sure that I was okay. "Need anything?" he sympathetically asked, looking at me with his chestnut eyes.

As he again sat on the edge of my bed, I refrained from running my fingers through his soft curly hair. There were so many things I wanted to do and say to him, but I remained content with the way things were and tried to show some restraint.

As if he knew what I was thinking, he leans in to kiss me.

"I know. You are definitely someone that I have grown to truly care about. I can see us being really happy one day. I just got to get you out of here first," he said, gently kissing my lips.

More determined than before, I made sure that Tracy brought the kids to me on a daily basis to help move my limbs when the therapists were seeing other patients.

As weeks passed, I started feeling things that I knew I had never felt since being hospitalized. I began feeling tingling sensations in my legs and feet and after the kids and Tracy finished therapy with me, I soon noticed more pain.

"Please don't get me wrong, because I don't want to give you false hope, but it seems that your paralysis may be reversible." Dr. Wilson said.

Without warning, an uncontrollable scream erupted from my mouth and tears followed. I had won the victory and was on my way to live the life I had deserved.

As he left the room to write orders for further testing, I let out a sigh and relaxed awhile since I knew there were better days were ahead.

The next morning I was taken down to radiology for an MRI. Upon my return, we prayed for a miracle. After hours had passed, Dr. Wilson entered the room with a look on his face that turned our hopes into disappointment.

As tears ran down my face, I waited for his response.

Looking at me in a way that I had not seen him look before, he walks towards the bed.

"Jaelynn, I cannot begin to tell you…" he hesitates before continuing.

"I don't know where to start. It's truly unbelievable."

With eyes wide open, impatience overcomes both Tracy and I. She stands and rushes to my bed.

"Please doctor...go on. Is it true? Is the paralysis reversible?" She begged with her hands clasped.

A smile overcomes his face, He answers yes.

He told us that it was not going to happen overnight, or even weeks for that matter, but with continuation of aggressive therapy, I would be able to eventually regain the function of my arms and legs.

We cried so much that our tears even got tired and dried up. Tracy called my parents as well as Monique and Jade and when they heard the news, they made her promise that she would call on a daily basis to give them an update of my status.

They said they would be on the first flight out when it was time for me to walk again, and to their surprise, they flew back to Kansas twenty three days later to walk by my side.

Although very weak, I looked forward to therapy as each day passed. I had made a miraculous recovery and looked forward to living the life that God had truly blessed me with.

"This too shall pass" were the words that kept replaying in my mind. Through tedious trials and tribulations, I overcame the odds and I made a promise to myself, God and my children that things were only going to get better.

Mind Games

ISEEMED TO have made a miraculous recovery despite what I had been through. As my body physically flourished, my mind seemed to go awry and I felt as if there were times that I was going insane.

I played it off when I felt as though I wasn't remembering the way that I used to. I would forget the simple things like what I had for dinner the previous day and the names of the nurses who had taken care of me for days at a time. I assumed that it was due to all of the medication that I was on and refused to tell anyone.

I believed that the stress of my life was finally catching up with me and instead of allowing it to get the best of me I attempted to ignore it while I focused on getting released.

With the aggravation of constantly being checked on by medical students, therapists, nurses and even visitors, I set aside at least ten minutes in the morning and evening to meditate and listen to whatever was being told to me. I felt it was what I needed in order to help block out the external stimuli that I thought was adding to my stress.

Days seemed to be getting better as I learned to speak up when I didn't feel like being bothered, but as time went on and they refused to speak of discharge plans, setbacks came into play.

I started hearing Brian speak to me as I began having vivid dreams that felt as if they were real.

"Baby, are you okay? Come on please talk to me, I'm right here," he begged as he fell to his knees beside me.

Instead of him lying on the floor the night we were shot, it was me. I tried to get up only to realize that I was almost lifeless. I tried to reach for him but my arms were as heavy as lead and I had no energy.

With barely enough air in my lungs to call out his name, I struggled to make a sound.

"Brian please help me."

Then, I passed out.

"Help me Brian, please don't leave." I moaned while forcefully wailing my arms and legs in bed.

As I continued to call out for him, a calming voice attempted to awaken me.

"Ms. Stone, wake up honey. You're having another dream." She said while placing a hand on my shoulder.

I jump up as if I didn't know her. It was just seconds later that I realized that she was the sitter that Dr. Wilson had ordered to stay with me since I was experiencing the vivid dreams that I had been encountering.

"Why are you looking at me like that?" I questioned while being embarrassed when I learned that she heard me moaning for Brian.

"I'm sorry, I was just concerned," she said.

"Well no need to be, it was just a dream. I'm fine. You can leave now."

Before attempting to go back to sleep, I apologized for my behavior and guaranteed that I would sleep throughout the remainder of the night.

At times when I was alone, I would often talk to him and apologize for the things that had happened. In fear, I also begged for him to let me be so I could move on with my life.

Tracy thought that I was losing it and warned me to stop discussing my thoughts with the nurses.

"Girl, trust me. You better keep your thoughts to yourself before they transfer you to the damn psych ward. You won't have to worry about going home," she threatened.

I couldn't believe she was talking to me as if there was something wrong with me, and in disgust I shot back at her trying to defend myself.

"I don't care what you or anyone else thinks. You of all people should know that I am not crazy! He's talking to me. He won't leave me alone. There's something I need to know!" I cried, not knowing what else to say.

Without saying a word, she stood to her feet and headed for the door.

Hoping that I didn't make her mad, I convince her to come back.

"Wait, where are you going? I'm sorry."

"Baby sis, me too. I just…I just want you to be careful about what you tell people. I'm looking out for your best interest, Jae." She apologizes as she hugs me.

"I'm going to get the babies. I'll be back."

She walks out the room.

That evening after dinner, I took a long shower, hoping it would relax my mind so I could be dream freely and prove to Dr. Wilson that I didn't need a babysitter. I had begged him to let me have one night without someone watching over me and that if I awakened in sweats that I would call the nurse myself for someone to come in to babysit me.

While taking my request into consideration, he relieved my evening sitter's post and replaced them with hourly room checks.

I went to bed early and slept without interruption. This time as I dreamt, I was at peace while Brian and I enjoyed each other's company. It was perfect, we were perfect and as I felt secure within his arms, I molded into him as if I were clay.

Within seconds, the dream once again turned vivid and I felt as if I was suffocating.

Trying to pry her small evil hands from around my neck, I continued to let out a silent scream. I couldn't breathe and the room started spinning. I forcefully kicked my legs as I tried to kick my female attacker. I began reliving the night that I was raped by Mike's friend and knew that I was fighting for a loss cause.

"Die, bitch." She whispered to my face as she continued choking me.

With piercing eyes she looked into mine as though she wanted to see the fear in them.

"You took away the man I loved. Now I'm taking your life. You should've already been dead."

She continued to choke the life out of me as my eyes watered helplessly, but when the nurse walked into to assess me, her hold was soon released.

"Get off of her! Help, I need help in her!" She yelled out as she began pulling Angie off of me.

While I attempted to reposition myself up in bed, I held my hands to my neck trying to soothe the pain I was feeling while gasping for air.

With a hoarse scream, I yelled out forgetting where I was.

"I've tried so hard to live again. How dare you try to take that away from me?"

As security escorted her out of my room, my eyes pierced into hers. If looks could kill, she would've been dead, and if it hadn't been for my hourly checks, I assume I would've been as well.

They took her to their holding office until the police arrived. When they arrived not only did I file charges for assault, but I also requested that Allen was paged so he could stay with me when he got off.

Standing over me with eyes blood shot red, I could tell he was exhausted. I needed his comfort, but also realized that he, too, got tired.

"Jae, I'm sorry I wasn't here for you." He softly spoke.

I wanted him to crawl in bed with me and comfort me like I wanted. But I knew that he needed rest and encouraged him to leave.

"It's okay. Thanks for coming." I said, biting my bottom lip.

"Go home. Get some rest, you're tired." I can see it in your eyes."

He stood there, before kneeling to his knees.

"Tell me," he said.

Looking at him as if I didn't know what he was talking about, I questioned him.

"Tell you what?"

"What you're thinking." He looked sadly into my eyes.

He knew me and was starting to know my thoughts. I wanted to tell him, but in fear of how he would feel, I hesitated before telling him.

"He's alive. I'm for certain now."

"Who?" he asked.

"Brian. I can feel it. I know it, Allen, and please don't think I'm crazy."

He knew I was serious and instead of having me elaborate any further, he told me okay and went home to get some rest.

I knew that because Brian was on my mind more than he wanted him to be, he decided to distant himself to give me space. Instead of visiting as often, he sent roses to take his place.

I became depressed and my appetite decreased as well. I refused to shower while also refusing therapy, and as time passed, I even discouraged Tracy from bringing my children to see me in fear that they would see me at my worst.

I was wasting away but this time didn't know how to come back.

My mom took the place of the frequent visit of the kids when I refused to let them see me.

For so many years, she felt that she was unable to give me the motherly advice that I needed, therefore she was determined to damn sure make it up.

"You are better than this Jaelynn Stone!" she scolded.

She was devastated and thought that if they had of been there for me instead of turning their backs on me, I wouldn't have ended up like this. She begged for me to get it together, reminding me that I had come too far.

"You are my child, so I know you are strong. You have no choice but to be," she reprimanded.

She recited the verse that I'll never forget, because she said it with so much hope and love:

"But they that hope in the Lord shall renew their strength, they shall take wings as eagles, they shall run and not be weary, they shall walk and not faint. That's from Isaiah 40:31."

She put my chin in the palm of her hands and as she looked at me and I at her, I felt the love that I had longed for all these years. Tears filled her eyes and I realized in that moment that I had never seen her as she was. At that point, I decided to keep pressing and living for my future.

New Beginnings

WITH THE love and encouragement that I was given by family, staff and even friends that I had made while in the hospital, I opened up and fought the depression I had encountered.

Unable to stay away, Allen apologized for the thoughts that he had, letting me know that he understood what I was going through.

"I can no longer be envious of Brian. He was a man that you loved and I have to respect that."

Without words being spoken, I smiled at him while letting him know that I too understood.

Brian was always going to remain a part of me regardless of whether he accepted it or not. Without Brian having been a part of my life, I was afraid of where I actually could have ended up.

He opened my eyes to things that I had never seen and for that I was grateful despite the outcome. I knew that everything happened for a reason and believed that without the drama that I encountered, I would have never meet Dr. Allen David.

After a long hospitalization, it was time for me to return home. The hospital had become my home away from home and before leaving, I made an attempt to say goodbye to those who changed my life.

Things were going to be drastically different for me, but I knew nothing was going to be impossible.

My family pulled together, making us all realize that life was too short to let minor things pull us apart from each other. From that point on, we cherished each day and spent many days together in an attempt to make up from lost times.

Being away from my children had not only matured them, but Tracy as well. Since she was their mother while I was away, she felt she needed to show them things that she as their step in mother should have shown awhile ago.

"Jae, meet Keith." She said as she backed up waiting for my approval.

With a smile on my face, I took in a deep breath.

"So he's the reason for this the new perfume?" I asked, as I let out a chuckle.

"Girl, you are so silly." she laughed.

Not knowing what to say, he stood to the side of her while holding her hand.

I was proud of her for becoming the adult that she needed to be. She deserved healthy love and a happy life.

Weeks after being home, I knew that I had to start doing things for myself without so much being dependent on others. I knew that I still had a long haul ahead of me, but I was determined to continue to get through it.

I began volunteering at community centers in the metropolitan areas in hopes that I would allow other women to see where life could take you if you didn't stand up for yourself.

I wanted to speak hope into the lives of the single sisters who were struggling to raise their children alone, letting them know that even if they had succumbed to the life that brought me to my knees, there was hope—and a way out.

I had learned a lot from the trials and tribulations that I had been through and felt that I could give back by lecturing to others who may have benefited from my advice.

"Love yourself before giving yourself away to those who won't love you back. Know that you are far better than what they are willing to give you," I said as they listened in awe.

Adrenaline rushed through my body as I pleaded with them.

"Whether you believe it right now or not, each and every one of you is worth more than anyone can imagine." Tears filled my eyes.

"Know that you are the only person who can keep you from showing your worth. You are the only person who can keep you from your dreams."

I was thankful for not only turning my life around but also for having the opportunity to inspire others.

No one would've ever imagined I'd be where I'm at in my life right now? I am now living a life filled with peace and harmony and letting God direct my path.

I had been through hell and back only realizing that if it wasn't for the road that led me to hell, I would've had no idea that this is where I was supposed to be.

I survived being broke, depressed, beaten, raped and even shot.

Being shot had left me lifeless, but with faith and determination, I survived physically, mentally, and spiritually.

Life is now worth living, and I am living the life I have always dreamed of. Without God placing me on my knees, I would've never been able to stand tall to be a witness for what He can do.

"So how do you feel right now?" he asked, as he held me in his arms.

With him giving me a gentle kiss to the side of my neck, chills ran through my body as I stared in the eyes that I had always loved to see.

He was indeed my soul mate and I knew it from the first day we met.

"I'm good. Real good." I said as I looked up at him.

"Thank you for being there for me." I said as I kissed him while realizing who he was to me.

As I placed my hand in his, tears began gently rolling down my cheeks while sniffles from our guests were heard throughout the room.

"Forever will I be the man for you. I'll love you endlessly because I belong to you," he said as he ended his wedding vow.

As I became Mrs. Allen David, I smiled, realizing that I married a man who was first my friend, lover then soul mate. In my heart, I knew that to him, I was not only his wife, but I was also the one who was beginning to change his life as drastically as he changed mine.

In him I had found a friend, in him I had found peace and in him I had finally found true love; but because of him I had found me and for that I was truly grateful and eternally blessed.